# THE
# CUERNAVACA
# QUESTION

*By Lydia Kirk*

# THE
# CUERNAVACA
# QUESTION

LYDIA KIRK

DOUBLEDAY & COMPANY, INC.
GARDEN CITY, NEW YORK
1974

All of the characters in this book are fictitious, and any resemblance to actual persons, living or dead, is purely coincidental.

ISBN: 0-385-06775-5
Library of Congress Catalog Card Number 73-11711
Copyright © 1974 by Lydia Kirk
All Rights Reserved
Printed in the United States of America
First Edition

*For Alice Stanley Acheson*

# THE
# CUERNAVACA
# QUESTION

The boy Pepe came out of the little hut at the back of the garden, his own hut. He slept there on a cot bed. The blankets were folded now, good blankets. Marta said the Señora had ordered them along with two pairs of cotton trousers, the pile of clean shirts, and the jug and basin in which he must wash. Carefully he took the jug and basin to the hose spigot behind the hut, scrubbed himself, and pulled a blue work shirt over his head. The white shirts were for evening or occasional lunchtimes when he carried drinks to the patio where the Señora entertained her guests. Returning to his hut for broom and rake, he started clearing leaves from beneath the flowering vines that grew over the garden walls. Too early yet, almost an hour too early, before he could go to the kitchen, where Marta would give him his morning coffee, too early to work near the house.

The sun showed a rosy light behind the distant gray mountains, then mounted swiftly into gold against a sky first pale, then deeper blue, until it reflected the even bluer water of the swimming pool in the patio beyond.

Pepe worked away. The sun was warm on his back. He swept the leaves into little piles, ducking under the crimson shower of bougainvillaea and cascades of orange and purple blossoms. He gave a look at the rose beds. The yellow bush had new blooms, enough to cut for the Señora's room. She liked yellow roses. Pepe admired the Señora as he admired the roses. He was very lucky to be working for her. Across the street his friend Beppo was not so fortunate. His master was a fat old man, pale and mottled like the toad who lived under the back garden gate, cross, too, always full of complaints. Yes, he, Pepe, was lucky.

There was Marta at the kitchen door. Laying his tools down, the boy went across the sunlit lawn through the stone passage into the kitchen where his bowl of coffee and a plate of fresh tortillas were set out on a wooden table. While he ate and drank, the woman and the boy chatted away until Conchita, the Señora's elderly maid, appeared, her arms full of linen on her way to the washhouse. Pepe was slightly in awe of Conchita who had a sharp tongue, but he knew she was good to the Señora. He spoke his *Bueno días* to her politely. She nodded, stopped to say a word to Marta, then went on. Later Pepe's Aunt Josefina would come by to pick up the bundle. The finer pieces Conchita washed herself, the hand-embroidered nightgowns, the underthings, lace-edged and delicate. When she returned Marta would have the Señora's tray set up and ready for her breakfast. Finishing his coffee, Pepe ran out to come back with one of the yellow rosebuds which he placed carefully in the little glass vase alongside the silver teapot, then he went to the front gate to pick up the morning paper, folded it neatly, and laid it also on the tray. He watched for a moment as Marta took toast from the oven, cut it and fitted the pieces into the rack next to a small jam jar. On a flowered plate she arranged strips of bacon and an egg, covering them with a glass bell. All was ready when Conchita came through again. Pepe thought the tray looked very pretty.

As Pepe went back to his work the early morning traffic sounded from the street outside the high brick walls. Once a quiet, sleepy town, Cuernavaca was now a city, ringed with small factories, shops of all kinds crowding its narrow streets and sidewalks, markets, cafes, souvenir stands on every corner. The old squares had been cleared, trees cut down around the grim pile that was Cortes's palace, and a wide expanse opened up for a parking lot where tourist buses discharged passengers from Mexico City. Only the rusted bandstand in a lower square and single knots of dark trees swarming with screaming birds, periling the old men sitting on benches underneath, remained shabby reminders of another day.

Still, Cuernavaca held enchantment for the well-to-do and fortunate Mexicans and foreigners who hid themselves behind walls to enjoy the famed climate of eternal spring and the fine views of the mountains from their windows and terraces, to enjoy life led at their own pace, in their own way, without much regard for the world behind the mountains. As in any contained society there was intrigue, jealousy, petty quarrels, dark corners at the edges of the sunlit gardens and ripples in the sparkling pools, but day after day bright light shone down to reassure the old and tired and sometimes to disturb any others bent on curious and devious purposes.

Calle Costanza, on the outskirts of Cuernavaca, had once been a dirt road. Now cars and trucks rumbled along its paved surface, avoiding an occasional cow or pig straying from the vacant lots still left between the houses and walled properties. Halfway down the street, behind its strong iron-studded wooden door, stood the Casa Santa Luiza, the home of the Señora Martínez. Once part of a convent, only the main section built around a patio and a small chapel on one side remained. The Señora, born Sara Sewall of Chicago, Illinois, had brought her Mexican husband here many years ago and had transformed the ruin into a beautiful home for the sick man, former ambassador in Rome, London, and the Vatican. Here he died very quietly in his room looking out over the flowered patio.

The Señora lived on, beloved, respected, feared by some, a great lady whose memories were walled in like her house. Not that the Señora lacked friends. She had many, some among the very poor whose angel of charity she became, others, admitted to her intimacy, were always welcome and she offered easy hospitality to any sent by solicitous friends abroad. Today she was entertaining at lunch. Marta told Pepe this, warning him to be ready to carry drinks to the patio. A small party, six, an American from the embassy with a young lady, Father Rodríguez, and another two, Dr. Hartung and his wife.

Father Rodríguez Pepe knew well. He lived next door in a small house, a good man, a great favorite of the Señora's. He did not dress like a priest, some said he had quarreled with the Church, with the former bishop, been cast out, but the people in the neighborhood loved him, brought their children to the classes he held on Saturday afternoons, let them go with him for walks in the country where he told them about the flowers and the rocks, about the sun and moon that rose over the mountains, and about the strange and faraway places where he had lived and traveled.

Dr. Hartung too was much interested in the rocks and caves, digging among old ruins and bringing back bits of bone and pottery to show the Señora. He and Father Rodríguez talked long of such things while the Señora sat and listened.

Now that his mistress was awake, Pepe could work nearer the house. He swept the patio, dusted the chairs, set clean ashtrays on the little tables, and filled the vases with fresh flowers, arranging them as she had taught him. All this done, he returned to the rose bed, carefully picking the best blooms which he carried in for Conchita to put in the Señora's room.

Just two years since Pepe had come to the Casa Santa Luiza. Hearing the Señora needed help in the garden, his aunt Josefina, the laundress, had brought him along. The eldest of her sister's family, Pepe had come to the city from their village on the Taxco road. Too many mouths to feed there, his aunt said; he was a good boy and quick, she'd find work for him in the town.

On Josefina's recommendation the Señora agreed to give Pepe a trial and turned him over to Guido, her old Italian servant who ruled house and garden. Guido was a stern taskmaster but a good teacher. The boy learned much in a year and a half and then Guido was gone, carried down to the cemetery at the foot of the hill, leaving the garden to Pepe's care while Conchita and Marta took charge of the house with occasional daily help. For special parties a very grand butler was called in, but otherwise they managed well enough. The house was not large, a long living room, a dining room, a small library where the Señora spent hours at her desk, her big bedroom next door, another, once her husband's, and the servants' quarters behind the kitchen. All the main rooms opened onto the patio, one section of which was roofed over against the sun.

Pepe was very happy, proud of his garden and pleased with the new tasks the Señora set him, carrying in drinks, even following Conchita with the vegetable dishes as she went around the table. Then, too, he was learning English. The Señora found books for him which he took across for lessons with Father Rodríguez. Now he could read and speak quite well. Perhaps one day he might even be taught to drive the fine old car that stood idle in a shed near the rear gate. That was his secret ambition and he pictured himself in a smart peaked cap like those of the chauffeurs who sat outside waiting for the Señora's most elegant guests.

A voice spoke from a door opened onto the patio.

"*Gracias*, Pepe, for the roses. They are very fine this year."

He looked up as the Señora walked out toward the swimming pool.

"Marta has told you there will be guests for lunch? If my American friends come early they may want a swim after the long drive from the city."

"*Sí, sí, señora.*" Pepe moved to take a long-handled net with which he fished the few stray leaves from the water. A struggling insect rose from the surface, shook its wings, then flew off into the sunshine.

The Señora came to stand by the boy. A tall thin woman, still erect on her cane, iron gray hair swept into a high pompadour above dark eyebrows and dark eyes, her silk dress hanging long around her ankles.

"Yes, the pool looks very nice, Pepe, the garden too."

She turned to walk slowly back into the house. Certainly there were days when she felt very old, but life here was tolerable enough, amusing too at times. Boredom she never permitted herself, "*accidei*," the Greeks called it, the one unpardonable sin. Even alone memories crowded in to savor and enjoy, and of memories she had enough to fill empty hours and sleepless nights.

She thought of the friends coming to lunch. For Father Rodríguez she felt real affection, a saintly man worn bone clean by his troubles. What an obstinate bigot the old bishop had been. She'd no patience with hypocrisy or vainglory. Dr. Hartung she found interesting. She liked his wife, a plain-faced intelligent woman, the young American from the embassy and Arabella Harris, always gay and charming. There were others she enjoyed seeing, the Russian princess who kept a silver shop in the town, Hugo, the bearded English artist, fine pictures he painted, many sent away to galleries abroad, the cheerful little bachelor who wrote endless unread books about rare birds and fishes, the occasional tourists sent to her by discriminating friends, even the single women she played bridge with on warm afternoons, fairly dull, most of them, but very restful.

Quite true, society in Cuernavaca was a queer mixture of the flotsam and jetsam tossed by life's currents into odd corners, Mexico, Greece, Portugal, Italy. There were the young men with soft voices and softer morals, the young women too, like butterflies moving from place to place, the dismal and forgotten old men and women come to hide their disappointments, the elderly retired couples living out the years, anxiously watching each other lest one be left alone, and all those widows, some brave, some silly. She shrugged, smiled, remembering she was a widow herself, but she'd been luckier than the rest. Yes, society in Cuernavaca was a mixed lot.

The morning wore on. Soon after twelve o'clock there was a loud noise of screaming sirens in the street outside the Casa. At the same time a bell clanged from the front gate, which Pepe ran to open for the Señora's American friends, Mr. Cooper and the pretty young lady, Miss Harris. The latter anxiously inquired for Señora Martínez.

"Seeing the ambulance, we were afraid, but the trouble seems to be next door."

Sure enough, police cars and an ambulance blocked the

roadway in front of Father Rodríguez's house, where a small crowd began to gather.

"No," stuttered Pepe, "the Señora is quite well, but . . ."

"She'll be disturbed by all this noise," broke in Miss Harris. "I'll go inside to find her. You two stay here."

She disappeared through the gate just as Father Rodríguez came out of his door, pushing between the uniformed men to bend over a huddled, bleeding form on the sidewalk. As Pepe and the American watched the excitement mounted and the crowd gathered closer, only to be shoved roughly back by the police. Swelling with importance, a postman came forward to speak with the captain in charge. He was the one to have given the alarm. He'd found this man lying on the sidewalk, knew he was dead by the look of him, the street empty, no one else around, so he'd rushed to the corner telephone booth and put in the call, then came back to wait for the police. No, he'd never seen the man before, didn't think he belonged in the neighborhood.

The Captain took the postman's name, then came to stand by Father Rodríguez. The priest finally rose as the body, now wrapped in a blanket, was laid on a stretcher and hoisted into the ambulance. For a moment the crowd was silent, then burst into loud chatter as the ambulance drove off. The Captain and Father Rodríguez went into the latter's house while others of the police circulated about asking questions of anyone who might have known the victim or seen his assailant. They approached the American gentleman who explained that he and his friend had just driven up, had been alarmed to find the police and ambulance in the street, fearing something might have happened to their hostess, Señora Martínez, who expected them for lunch. Pepe, very frightened, said he had come to answer the Señora's bell and open the gate. No, he'd not been outside since early morning, then only to pick up the newspaper.

Pursuing their questions, the police went from house to house. Deliveries had been made, cars driven out, trash collected, the ordinary morning routine, but no one volunteered help or information, nor had anyone noticed the man on the sidewalk until the police arrived. Stood to reason he could not have lain there very long, passing cars or someone besides the postman would certainly have seen him.

Gradually the crowd melted away. Most of the police left, two or three remaining to wait for the Captain, still in conference with Father Rodríguez. Satisfied there was nothing more to learn the American motioned Pepe inside the Casa gate. Pepe was relieved as the wooden door shut behind them. He was still frightened, very frightened, because, from the glimpse he had had of the man on the sidewalk, he thought he had seen him somewhere, at some time, not here, somewhere else. But this he had not told the police; it was nothing, perhaps only a dream. Avoiding the kitchen where Josefina the laundress had just arrived with the news, embellished now with every lurid detail, Pepe went quietly to his little hut to change into white shirt and clean trousers, then came back to the patio to set out glasses and bottles ready for the luncheon drinks.

The Señora, greatly agitated, was walking about the garden with the two Americans. Calling to Pepe she asked anxiously after Father Rodríguez.

"What a dreadful thing, terrible it should have happened right here in front of the Father's house. Did he go along with the ambulance?"

"No, señora, after it left the Father and the police captain went inside his house."

"You say no one recognized the dead man?"

"I don't think so, señora. The police questioned everyone."

"Certainly none of us were out this morning," then remembering, "When you picked up the paper, was the man lying there?"

Pepe shook his head. "I saw nothing, señora."

She turned to the Americans. "I do hope this won't make trouble for Father Rodríguez. Perhaps he may tell us something when he comes to lunch."

The bell rang again, this time for Dr. and Mrs. Hartung, who came in, horrified when told of the morning's tragedy. Like the Señora they were very concerned for Father Rodríguez, such a good man, often coming out to the dig on the Taxco road where the Norwegian archaeologist was working.

"We are making progress, señora, but we go slowly. Nothing much found so far, only a few bits of pottery like those I showed you, and some broken tools. The experts at the museum are doubtful, yet there are new indications . . ." The Doctor proceeded to discuss various aspects of soil and rock, the layers to be gone through and sifted, and the dating and cataloguing of the pottery.

The Señora listened patiently, her mind still full of anxiety for her friend next door.

Conchita came to ask if the Señora wished luncheon to be served.

"We will wait a little longer, though I know you must be hungry, Mr. Cooper, and Arabella here will be due back at her shop."

"Please, don't bother about me, señora, my customers are late shoppers."

As she spoke Father Rodríguez came up the path from the back gate, a tall man with a white drawn face, a high-bridged nose, fine eyes, and thinning gray hair. "My apologies, I'd hoped you had gone in without me." Greeting the Señora and her guests, still standing, he accepted a drink. "Don't let me keep you."

The Señora looked up at him, sensing he did not wish to speak of the morning's events, so she rose to her feet and ushered her guests into the cool tile-floored dining room. Taking their cue from her, the company talked of this and that, Dr. Hartung entertaining with stories of archaeological exploits and Arabella describing the difficulties of fitting stout American tourist ladies into unlikely Mexican fiesta costumes and their husbands into flowered shirts, sombreros and serapes. The lunch was good, though neither the Señora nor the priest ate with much appetite.

As it was late the guests did not sit long over coffee. Father Rodríguez took Dr. Hartung aside for a few moments, after which the latter, pleading an appointment, excused himself to the Señora and left with his wife. Mr. Cooper and Arabella got up to follow. The Señora walked with them to the gate, said good-by, urging them to come back another day for the promised swim.

Once outside, the gate shut behind them, Arabella turned to her escort. "What really happened out here, Henry? I'm simply bursting with curiosity. Everyone was so cautious at lunch."

"I must say we were all very discreet. A knifing on the priest's doorstep can't be an everyday occurrence."

"The man was dead, wasn't he?"

"Quite dead. A stranger apparently, unless Father Rodríguez identified him to the police captain when they went into the house. The police questioned everyone in the crowd, didn't seem to get much satisfaction. No one saw the man on the sidewalk until a passing postman reported it."

"What kind of a man was he? You think the Father knew him?"

"He looked like a workman of sorts, poor clothes. The killer did a thorough job, pretty messy. Curious business. If the Father knew him he certainly kept very silent about it."

"You never met Father Rodríguez before?" asked the girl. "He's a quiet, kind man. I don't believe he has an enemy in the world, except the old Bishop, and bishops don't strew corpses on doorsteps because they disapprove a priest's opinions. More likely the man himself had enemies, came to the Father for help. He's always picking up lame ducks, or the man may have committed a crime and wanted to confess."

"Maybe, but it's queer all the same."

They walked down the street toward the parked car. All now seemed relatively peaceful. "Must you really go back to your shop?" This girl was attractive, an unlikely find here in Cuernavaca, bright brown hair, blue eyes, a good figure, a mouth that curled engagingly at the corners. Henry hated to lose her so quickly.

"But of course I must go back. Come along if you like, I'll sell you a serape."

"Seriously, why not play hooky just for this afternoon," he asked.

Arabella shook her head. "Can't be done."

"Don't you ever take time off?"

"The odd Sunday, yes, Friday and Saturday are busy days, and this, Mr. Cooper, is Friday."

"Anyway, I'll see you to your shop. I'm interested in those serapes."

They got into Henry Cooper's car and drove out onto the main road. Here fine stone walls, some with imposing gates, shut the large houses from view, but there were patches of miserable rubble where goats grazed and ragged children played around tin-roofed huts. Henry swerved to avoid a stray cow that wandered across the road.

"Not much town planning in Cuernavaca," he commented.

"No, but there's a kind of horrid charm about it all, contrasts of rich and poor, sunlight and dirt."

"What brought you to Cuernavaca?" Henry asked the girl.

"Escape, the usual thing. I'd been working in New York, drifted down here a year ago."

The young man started to say something, thought better of it, warned off by the note in her voice.

They rode on for some minutes in silence.

"Take a right turn here," Arabella directed, "around the palace square. The shop is in the arcade over there, across from the fountain. Here's the parking lot. But you really don't want a serape. I'll say good-by now. Thank you for the lift."

"You can't believe how badly I need a serape. Besides there's lots to talk about, the Señora, the priest, the murder mystery. Our meeting is only a first chapter."

The girl laughed. "Come along, then. Serve you right if I make you model a sombrero for the first tourist."

Threading their way out of the square past eager little boys selling straw bags and shoelaces, old beggar women, innumerable curio stands, newspaper kiosks, and a large open cafe, they finally entered the brightly lighted arcade, where, halfway down, Arabella stopped in front of her boutique, empty except for the stout proprietress, Mrs. Harvey, to whom she presented Henry Cooper.

Mrs. Harvey, amply arrayed in a splendid creation of flowered silk, greeted the young man with approval and proceeded to lay out a selection of colored shirts for his inspection.

"You're stealing my customer, Mrs. Harvey," objected Arabella. "It's a serape he wants."

"Meanwhile I'll settle for this blue job."

"And very becoming to a blond young man," said Mrs. Harvey, holding up one of the plainer shirts with figured collar and cuffs.

"This too," Henry indicated with a bow to Arabella as he handed over the brightest of the serapes, red and green with a horrendous border of black snakes. "A present for my young nephew in Boston. He'll be delighted."

Arabella laughed, made a face as Mrs. Harvey went off to make up the package and take change from the cash drawer in her desk.

"What about Sunday?" Henry asked. "We might drive out to the Doctor's dig, have lunch on the way. I've never seen the place. Who knows, our second chapter may be as interesting as the first."

Arabella hesitated. "You go very fast, Henry."

"Come along. We might find Cortes's treasure ourselves. I'll stop by for you. Same address the Señora gave me today?"

"Suppose it rains."

"It never rains in Cuernavaca. I'll be there around eleven."

Picking up his package, he said good-by to Mrs. Harvey without waiting for Arabella's answer and was out the door.

The proprietress looked after him. Such a pleasant young man, so right for this nice girl, who seemed to have few friends of her age here in town. Nor in the year she'd worked in the shop had she confided to Mrs. Harvey her reason for coming to Mexico. Too strict a family at home? A disappointed love affair more likely, but, the old woman thought to herself, young hearts mended quickly, especially a heart belonging to anyone as pretty as Arabella.

A party of eager tourists arrived and the two women were soon busy attending to their wants—blouses, the inevitable

1

lace-trimmed dresses, and odd bits of colored pottery to be chosen and wrapped.


After the young people left the Casa Santa Luiza, Señora Martínez and Father Rodríguez sat on alone in the patio. Neither said anything for several minutes. Finally the Señora reached to the table beside her, took a cigarette from a silver box, and lighted it.

"The man who was killed, did you know him, Carlos?"

"No. At first he reminded me of one of the workmen from Hartung's dig, but then again . . ." The priest's hands moved uncertainly along the arms of his chair. "I don't know. He was an Indian type, like so many others."

"You spoke with the Doctor before he left?"

"He knew nothing. His workers come and go."

"The police questioned you?"

"Yes, but what could I tell them? I'd no wish to involve our good Doctor because a man attacked on the street had fallen in front of my house, then too, if that man was coming to see me, if he was in trouble, all the more reason to say nothing even if I had recognized him."

"True, Carlos, you've never turned a man, woman, or child in need away from your door. But this killing seems strange."

The priest smiled. "Señora, we Mexicans are a violent people. Blood is easily spilled, tempers flare, knives are drawn, even small quarrels can result in tragedy."

The Señora held her hand out to the priest. "I hope this won't mean trouble for you, Carlos."

"Dear lady, one more trouble will add little to the burden I carry already. And now I must not keep you from your siesta."

"You will let me know if there is news?"

Father Rodríguez shook his head. "Life here is bought and sold very cheap. I doubt if we hear any more of the affair."

Still concerned for her friend, the Señora watched him as he walked slowly down the path to the back gate. Yes, he had known much trouble, his own and that of others. His own courage and faith sustained him as it sustained the simple people who came to him for help. Courage she did not lack, but she envied him his faith.

The hot afternoon sun shone down on the open patio and laid fingers of light through the slotted section where Pepe came to gather up coffee cups, glasses, and bottles. He carried them inside, then straightened the chair cushions and emptied the ashtrays. He looked about to make sure all was in order before going across the garden to his hut. There he changed into his work clothes, then, picking up his English grammar and exercise book, he went to sit under the tree that arched shade over the back gate. Later he must go to Father Rodríguez to recite his lesson, but his mind was full of uneasy thoughts and the words blurred as he turned the pages of his book. The face of the man on the sidewalk swam before his eyes, a clouded vision of something, someone, seen before. He wished he might talk about it with his friend Beppo, but this was a kind of secret thing and, besides, he'd not seen Beppo today. The fat man's house was shut. He'd noticed that as he stood in the street. The gates were bolted and no one from the house had come out into the crowd.

Just then the toad, the toad that looked like the fat man, hopped out from its hole by the gate, gobbled up an insect, and sat blinking at Pepe. Horrid creature. The boy moved over, out of his sight, wondering again where Beppo had gone and how he could bear working for the fat man.

Saturday came and went. The police did not return to Calle Costanza. Father Rodríguez took a party of children to see the ruined pyramid on the edge of town near the railway tracks. The Señora lunched at home. Three friends came to play bridge, and Pepe helped serve them tea, iced drinks, and little cakes.

On the Sunday, his monthly day off, Pepe dressed in his good clothes, added a necktie to his shirt, and caught the bus into town. His aunt Josefina was waiting for him outside the cathedral door, and together they went into the dim old church, now rapidly filling for the noonday Mass. Josefina pushed along through the crowd until they found seats toward the center front. This was important, for her husband played in the mariachi band, the group of folk musicians who accompanied the Mass. They were coming in now, each man carrying his instrument, drums, guitars, gourd rattles, flutes, and odd-looking old fiddles. Josefina was very proud of her husband, the stout red-faced carpenter and stonemason who flourished sticks over a small colored drum.

Pepe watched as the men took their places at the foot of the chancel and the clergy in procession marched up the aisle. Incense curled in gray puffs as they came by, headed by the Bishop in robes and mitre, crook in hand.

The Mass began, the musicians playing at intervals, the rattle of the gourds and the drumbeats accenting the rhythm. Ordinarily Pepe loved these sounds, his body swaying to the music. Today he scarcely heard them. Instead he looked up at the frescoes on the cathedral wall. Once they had been whitewashed over in revolutionary days, but the new Bishop had had them cleaned and restored. Father Rodríguez had told Pepe the story of the Mexican missionaries who went to Japan four hundred years ago, only to be captured and crucified. The frescoes pictured them on their crosses, a row of crosses, one after the other. This morning the martyrs looked down on the boy, more real to him than any of the people beside him in the church.

The Bishop was finishing his sermon. Soon the Mass would be over. Aunt Josefina and his uncle would take him home to their little house. There would be a hot meal, big bowls of chili beans and stewed meat and the sweet cake Josefina knew Pepe liked. He must not think of the dead man on the sidewalk. He would pray for him; that was all he could do.

Pepe knelt for the Bishop's blessing. The musicians packed up their instruments and the crowd filed out into the sunshine, children running ahead to buy the spun sugar sticks sold at the churchyard gate.

The town was very crowded. Postcard sellers, the boys loaded with their straw bags, stood on every corner to attract Sunday tourists. Souvenir shops and cafes around the main square were wide open as Pepe, his aunt, and his uncle pushed their way along to a bus stop, turning aside for a small procession headed by a band, a saint's banner held high, followed by a straggle of men women and children carrying drooping flowers on their way to a local shrine.

The bus rattled across town to the stop near Josefina's house. She hurried the other two down the street and bustled them inside while she clattered pans in the little back kitchen and told Pepe to set plates and bowls ready on the scrubbed wooden table. Throughout the meal Pepe sat quietly while his aunt and her husband talked away. She was still full of yesterday's drama, wished she had seen the poor man before he was carted off in the ambulance. Queer no one recognized him, but there were a lot of drifters about looking for work in the town.

"That reminds me. Dr. Hartung told Marta he needed an extra man at the digging. One of his walked off a couple of days ago. It's not hard work, just shoveling dirt about. I can't think why they make such a fuss over the broken bits they pull out, besides"—she crossed herself—"they say there's a curse on the place."

Her husband grunted over his bowl of chili.

"Some say it's treasure he's looking for. Fine lot of treasure in those broken pots. Waste of time, I call it, but the Doctor pays good money. That no-account Pedro Herrera, who married the Bastina girl, they say he's buying a car, a big one, must have cost him a pretty penny, and there's others in the village, drinking their pay up most of them."

"You talk too much, Josefina." Her husband pushed his bowl to one side and helped himself to stew.

Pepe listened, said nothing.

"What's the matter with you, boy?" his aunt asked. "Lost your tongue as well as you appetite? You've left half your food on your plate."

Pepe took a few more mouthfuls. It was good stew, but today it seemed to stick in his throat, and besides all that about the Doctor and the digging made him uneasy. He remembered Pedro, a big bully of a man who used to frighten the children in his village. Pepe knew, of course, that many men, and even some of the older village boys, were working at the digging, but if Pedro was cheating the Doctor, the Señora's friend, that was very bad. Pepe had not been back to his old home for some months. Perhaps Beppo from the house across the street could tell him something. He'd said last week his master was sending him to Taxco and he would stop off for a word with Pepe's family. No sign of Beppo yesterday, however, so he must still be away.

His mind somewhat at rest, Pepe ate a large piece of the sweet cake Josefina set before him, scraping up the last crumbs, but he made excuses to go off soon after lunch. He wanted to get back to the Casa on the chance Beppo might have returned.


Promptly at eleven that Sunday morning Henry called at Arabella's door. She came out looking fresh and pretty in a yellow cotton dress, a scarf tied round her dark hair.

"You're sunshine itself," he said. "It's a glorious day. I thought we might lunch at the Vista del Rey. They've a pool there. We could have that swim we missed on Friday."

"What fun, I've never been to the Vista. Just a minute, I'll run back for my suit."

They got happily into his car, parked dangerously in the narrow street but watched by a band of ragged urchins to whom Henry distributed a handful of coppers. Out through the town, threading their way past the trippers buses and the pushing Sunday crowds, they were soon on the main Taxco highway.

"If you don't mind we'll turn off, take the old road, it's a bit rough but we'll avoid the holiday traffic and it's shorter to the Vista this way."

Beyond Cuernavaca a fertile valley ran for several kilo- meters, fields of waving green sugar cane alternating with wide stretches of corn, here and there groves of olive and fruit trees and patches of the spiky plants from which strong bitter liquor is distilled.

Once part of huge estates held by the old hacienda pro- prietors, the land was now subdivided, some of it in government co-operatives, smaller acreages farmed by village groups, some few by individuals. There were not many single holdings, houses standing alone in the fields, Mexicans preferring to huddle together in settlements from which they rode out to work in trucks, on horseback or astride their burros. Today, Sunday, the fields were nearly empty, the men gathered in groups outside the village wineshops, the children playing in the dirt around the tin- or tile-roofed adobe shanties. In the small market booths set up along the road women in black or colored *rebozos* haggled and gossiped as they fingered the pottery jugs and cheap finery and filled their baskets with vegetables and fruit. Goats, pigs, and chickens roamed about, a hazard to driving. The car swerved as a ragged child ran out holding up an iguana by the tail.

"Stewed lizard for lunch, or would you like it dried and stuffed for your living room?"

Arabella shuddered. "Nasty things. The country people catch them in the rocks and tourists actually buy them."

A sign at a corner pointed the way down a long avenue to the Vista del Rey. Once a great hacienda belonging to one of Cortes's lieutenants, some said even to Cortes himself, the main building had been converted into a resort hotel. A large swimming pool occupied part of the central courtyard with outbuildings around it arranged as individual cottages. A restaurant, opening on the court, was set in the old cellars below the main floor. Here crops, sugar and corn, had once been stored in the arched alcoves, the front part now railed off and set with rustic tables and chairs. Gardens stretched beyond the pool and groups of holiday guests sat about enjoying the sun which poured down over beds of bright flowers.

The water was blue and cool. Henry and Arabella swam, came out to sit along the edge, and swam again.

"Delicious. Makes one forget Cuernavaca crowds, all the

tourist claptrap," said the girl as, almost reluctantly, they went in to change. But later, when they found chairs and a table under a tree and ordered long cold drinks, both agreed the world could indeed be a pleasant place.

"Tell me, Henry," asked Arabella. "What's your job at the embassy?"

There was a pause as a waiter set food down before them.

"I'm an attaché, a general sort of handyman, filling in here and there."

"I know you speak very good Spanish and you get around a lot. I imagined you might be some kind of intelligence officer."

"I suppose we all do a bit of that. Mexican affairs are pretty complicated. The government is stable enough, but there are always rascals around. Our ambassadors travel with armed guards. We have to keep our ears to the ground."

And that, thought Arabella, was a very neat way of side-stepping my question.

"As for my Spanish. I grew up in Chile and Brazil. My father was a mining engineer. I went back to the States for school and college, tried my hand at engineering when I got out, but it wasn't any good. Father had retired, taken the family home to live. I'd always enjoyed foreign travel, had a wandering foot, so I applied for the service. My languages helped, Spanish, Portuguese, and the German I learned from an old tutor. Lots of Germans in Chile at one time. So, there's the story of my life. What about yours?"

"Nothing so romantic, I'm afraid. I was born in New York, went to the usual schools, to college, did the usual social things, decided in the usual way my family did not understand me, so I went to Paris, studied design there for a year, came home, took a job, lived with the usual girl friend in the usual walk-up flat, and," reaching out to take a flower from the vase on the table, she looked up at Henry for a moment, "had the usual unhappy sort of affair and here I am, the usual escapee."

"And so you decided to cut loose from the usual. But why Cuernavaca?"

"Friends told me of a job here. It's a step on the road—to where I'm not sure. But don't you agree, there's a kind of horrid fascination about the place?"

"Aren't you afraid it may trap you?" Henry asked.

"How could it? The world behind these mountains is too wide."

"True enough. Meanwhile, if you've finished we'd best push along to the dig."

As they left their table and walked up the stone steps to the main floor, Henry called Arabella's attention to the cellars that stretched into darkness beyond the cleared restaurant area.

"Easy to imagine those old Spaniards using this as a kind of fortified place, storing gunpowder as well as sugar."

"Or using it to shut up their prisoners. I know there was fighting in these parts during the revolutions, perhaps even earlier. Cortes and his men must have been a rough lot."

Arabella stopped to look out through the arches to where sunlight shone on children playing in the pool. Suddenly she shivered. "Yes, Mexico is like this, always those contrasts of light and shadow. Never mind, the light was lovely today, luncheon was great fun, Henry. I'm so glad we came."

Back in the car they drove down the avenue and turned right. The road climbed toward the mountains, rocks and tufts of gray-green cactus, only here and there small patches of corn. They rode on for some way, talking of this and that, of friends in Cuernavaca and in the City.

"That was a queer business last Friday, wasn't it, Henry?"

"I'd hoped you'd forgotten it."

"No, I've thought about it a lot. Señora Martínez was really disturbed, and poor Father Rodríguez. It was all quite horrid."

"I agree it's not pleasant to have a dead man on your doorstep, but such things have even happened in New York. The world is full of violence these days."

"Yes, but why should it happen there in that quiet street? Don't you think it odd yourself?"

"The police were very much on the job. Perhaps they will come up with something."

"Perhaps, and perhaps not. Mexican police are . . . Mexicans. Anyway I'm curious."

Henry said nothing, nor could he tell her he had made discreet inquiries in Mexico City where certain individuals in Cuernavaca were already being investigated. He also had been disturbed by Friday's events, so much so he could not believe that the workman's stabbing was a casual occurrence. So far there seemed no real clues and the dead man was still unidentified. Like Arabella and the Señora he could hardly think the priest, Father Rodríguez, was involved. True, he had noticed him talking with Dr. Hartung before they left the Casa Santa Luiza, but that could mean nothing.

In front of them the road dipped suddenly, unexpectedly, into a small sheltered valley where a few houses clustered around an open square. Only children seemed about at this hour; one holding the inevitable iguana by the tail shouted as they drove past. Just a little distance from the houses, over the sparse treetops, was the squat tower of a church. Circling the square, they came out into a dusty lane that ended where a sprawling wooden fence enclosed the churchyard area.

An old live oak tree stood beside a pair of wide gates, and

beneath it, in the shade, a hunched man sat asleep wrapped in his serape.

Henry and Arabella got out of the car.

"This can't be the place, Henry. No sign of a dig here."

"Looks unlikely, doesn't it, but wait . . ." He tried the gate fastened with a rusted lock and chain, then went over to the Mexican who grunted and rose slowly to his feet.

"We are friends of Doctor Hartung."

The man shook his head. "Visitors not allowed. Everything shut today."

Henry felt in his pocket, jingling a few coins.

"The American Señorita wishes to see the church. The Doctor, our friend, has told us about it. We only want to look around."

The man looked at Henry, who jingled the money in his pocket again, then he shrugged and shuffled toward the gate, producing a key on a long chain. Henry motioned to Arabella, thanked the Mexican, and put the coins into his hand. The man peered after them as they went through, then went back to sleep again under the tree.

Arabella laughed. "A fine lot of security if the dig is really here."

"A few pesos undo most locks," Henry answered. "First we'll look around the church, just in case the old boy wakes up."

They crossed what was more meadow than churchyard. The grass under their feet was soft and spongy.

"Must be water somewhere about," remarked Henry.

The church door stood half open. Inside the building was cool and empty, unused by the look of it. Overhead the roof beams were rotted and there was a pervasive smell of damp decay. Some broken rush-bottomed chairs were stacked against the walls. Guttered candles in rusted tin holders stood on the altar below a flaked primitive painting of an emaciated, tortured Christ.

Instinctively Arabella took Henry's hand and together they went out again into the sunshine.

"Not a cheerful place, but if I'm right the dig must be close by. Let's explore furthur."

The ground rose sharply behind the church, and below, off to one side, was a grove of dark trees. Here, sure enough, a small stream trickled down from overhanging rocks, then lost itself amid thick reeds and seeped into the meadow grass. Just beyond, through the treetops, Henry and Arabella could see a group of new wooden huts. Picking their way over flat stones that made a bridge across the stream, they came out through the trees and climbed up the slope to the huts. As they came closer, the door of the middle hut opened and a big rough-looking man, a heavy-faced Indian type, came out. He pointed to a sign, "*No Pase.*"

Henry went forward. "We are friends of Doctor Hartung."

Shaking his head, the man barred the way.

"The Doctor is not here."

"Perhaps then you could show us around." Once more Henry put his hand into his pocket, but the man stood immovable.

"No visitors allowed."

"We'd best go back, Henry," said Arabella, "or you'll have a fight on your hands. He looks ugly and I think he's drunk."

Henry hesitated. The man took a step toward them, shouted something as another, smaller man, came up behind.

"Retreat's indicated, I'm afraid. Don't run. I'll keep an eye on our friends as we go down." Walking slowly, Henry took Arabella's hand and led her back, the two men watching them from above.

In the car again Henry took the direct road to Cuernavaca. They rode quietly along, both full of their own thoughts. Arabella was disturbed by unbidden, unsought feelings. The New York episode had left her numbed and hurt, but today she had begun to realize life held much that was new and exciting. As she and Henry had lunched and walked down the hill hand in hand, she sensed there might be a beginning to something as yet undefined, a faint stirring for which she was grateful.

Henry too was attracted to the girl, but he felt she must be approached slowly, warily, lest she take fright. He did not know whether this day had meant as much to her as it had to him, nor did he know how deep the old hurt had been, but he was determined to see more of her, hopefully to break through the reserve with its occasional bitter memories of the past. So, after he let her out in front of her house, he leaned over, kissed her, then turned quickly away as he watched her go through the door and up the stairs to her flat.

As Pepe got off the bus Sunday afternoon and started up the hill, he noticed a number of parked cars just beyond the turning into Calle Costanza. From one of them two men in city clothes got out, walked down the street, and stopped in front of the Fat Man's house. Pepe hurried after them, hoping for a sight of Beppo if he came to open the door, but the men entered quickly and the door shut behind them. The shutters of the house were still closed tight, but Pepe thought he heard voices from the walled garden. A minute later Beppo wheeled a bicycle through a side gate. Pepe crossed the street.

"When did you get back?"

"Last night late."

"You missed a lot. Did you hear what happened Friday morning?"

Beppo turned his head. "The men in there were talking about it."

"Those men that just went in?"

"Yes, and some others. They're drinking in the back garden, having a big discussion. They've run out of bottles. I'm going down the hill to the store to bring more back. No time now, but I've got lots to tell you. I stopped in the village on the way back from Taxco."

"Can you come over this evening, Beppo? I'll be in the hut."

"I'll try. The men should be gone then, or drunk."

Beppo was two years older than Pepe, almost a man in Pepe's eyes. Never overbright in his lessons, Beppo had been Pepe's classmate at school and he had always befriended Pepe, fought for him against bigger boys, taught him tricks of defense, never teased him because he was more interested in his studies than the others, even showed a kind of brotherly pride in Pepe's progress with Father Rodríguez and the Señora. Pepe never understood why Beppo was satisfied to work for the Fat Man, but Beppo was cheerful, easygoing, took things as they came, and of course the pay was good.

Crossing back to the Casa, Pepe went around and let himself in at the back garden gate. The house was quiet. There was nothing much for him to do, but he got out the hose, watered some of the beds, and gave a look to the roses. Plenty there for fresh vases tomorrow, so he went into the kitchen, where Marta, on her day off, had left bread, cheese, and fruit on the table for his supper.

It was ten o'clock before Beppo knocked on the Casa's back gate.

"I'd given you up."

"Those men. What a lot of talk and drink. One's left in the garden, passed out, the others finally cleared off, and the Master's gone to bed."

Pepe produced two bottles of Coke given him by his aunt, and perched himself on his cot, Beppo settling into the hut's one chair.

"That Taxco bus was full Thursday, crying babies and fat old women falling over each other when we went around the curves. Some of the children were sick, awful mess. I had a package to deliver, had trouble finding the right house and street, but the man gave me a good tip. After that—you remember Luis, used to live in our village? He keeps a cafe in Taxco now, nice old man. He treated me to dinner and a bed, asked after you. Anyway I had to wait around all next day for some letters to bring back here, so I got a late bus and stopped off at the old home. Boy, did they give me a good meal, Pepe."

"Did you see any of my people?"

"Your father came by. He looks all right, said to tell you your mother and the kids were fine, only stayed for a minute. After he'd gone some of the men who work at the Doctor's dig turned up. There was a lot of talk, seems there's been trouble there, fights going on behind the Doctor's back. That big guy Pedro has been swelling around as if he owned the place. He made a pass at another guy, that fellow who came up fom Puebla, had a real set-to and the man's not been heard of for days."

"Beppo, what did the Puebla man look like?"

"Not tall, kind of thick, like a lot of those Puebla people."

Pepe's eyes grew bright and round. "I remember, didn't we see him last Christmas when we were in the village together?"

"Might have."

"What was his name?"

"Pablo something or other."

"That's the man, I'm sure . . ."

Pepe stopped short. Beppo was his friend, but could he tell him, dared he tell him, the crazy thought that had just come into his head?

"Go on, Beppo, was there anything more?"

"Only some say there's stuff being stolen from the dig, though I can't see who'd want those old broken pieces. Anyway you can be glad none of your people work there. Too much talk. I'd heard enough so I went off to bed, fooled around next day, and took the afternoon bus back here. Too bad I missed the excitement Friday morning. Who found the man on the sidewalk, by the way?"

"The mailman. He called the police. They came with an ambulance. By that time everyone had come out into the street, a big crowd. The police asked a lot of questions, went to all the houses, but no one had seen or heard anything. They took the body away. No news since then."

"Queer, wasn't it? Well, it's late. I'll go along, see if that fellow is still sleeping it off in the garden."

Pepe let Beppo out the gate, bolted it, and came back to the hut. As he undressed and lay down on his cot, he thought over all Beppo had said, thought and wondered why he'd not told Beppo the dead man reminded him of someone he'd seen before. He'd held back, just why he didn't know. He felt suddenly very afraid, for if the dead man was really Pablo, he, Pepe, must tell someone, not the police, he would be too scared, not Marta or his aunt, not even the Señora, too great a lady to be bothered. No. Pepe's mind went round and round. It was all too much, his head ached and he was very tired, so tired he slept until dreams came to frighten him again. He

woke and knew there was only one person to whom he could
go, Father Rodríguez.

Señora Martínez rarely accepted invitations, preferring to
entertain friends at home, so Conchita was surprised on Monday morning when her mistress ordered a bag to be packed,
and Ector told her she was driving to the city. Conchita's
cousin Ector kept a garage in town and obliged when the
Señora needed a chauffeur, now the old Italian Guido was
gone. Ector even had a uniform pressed and ready for just
such occasions and he came by regularly to keep her car in
order, the fine Bentley brought back from Europe, stately
and well bred as the Señora herself.

"I will wear the black lace, Conchita. There is a dinner at
the American Embassy this evening. We spend the night as
usual at the hotel. If I am not too tired we return tomorrow."

"But, señora," Conchita looked her disapproval. "After so
much excitement here last week the Señora should rest."

"Nonsense. A little outing will be good for us both. The
Ambassador called this morning. I had sent regrets, but he
insisted. Get along, Conchita. Ask Pepe to wash and polish
the car so it will be ready for Ector. We will leave at two
o'clock. Tell Marta to give me an early lunch."

Conchita shook her head, set her lips in a straight line as
she went out to relay the Señora's orders. Experience taught
her there could be no argument when the mistress took sudden decisions, but she had no hesitancy in voicing her opinion
to Marta. The latter, however, shrugged her shoulders.

"It is long since the Señora has been to one of the grand
city parties. She is right to go. It will be a change, besides"—
Marta gave Conchita a shrewd look—"think how you like to

see her dressed up, diamonds and all. Not much chance here for that sort of thing."

Still grumbling, only half mollified, Conchita went out to find Pepe. Marta smiled, knowing of the old maid's real devotion to the Señora and of her pride in her appearance, for which Conchita would take full credit. No fear of complaints when they returned next day. Conchita would come back pleased with the whole affair.

Pepe was delighted to be told to clean the Señora's car. He went out immediately with pail, rags, and polish and soon had it shining like new. Ector had taught him just how it should be done, and he worked happily away. He had wakened this morning still fearful after the night's dreams but determined to find a chance to confide in Father Rodríguez. Now, with the Señora gone to the city, it would be easy and somehow he felt the Father would make everything right.


Ector drove smoothly, Conchita sitting rigidly straight beside him, her hands clasped over the Señora's jewel case. In the cushioned back of the old limousine Señora Martínez closed her eyes. She slept as they came down through rocky mountain passes and out into the valleys, spreading corn and maguey fields on either side. As they climbed again and neared the city she wakened and leaned forward to make sure the windows were tight shut against the choking yellow dust set up by the factories that lined the road.

Mexico City, in a bowl surrounded by mountains, suffers pollution that only disappears in the autumn rains and winds. Today it seemed particularly bad. The traffic, too, was heavy and grew worse as they came into the center of the city. No wonder, she thought, people were moving out into the suburbs, the fine old houses pulled down or converted into commercial use. She still remained faithful to the Old Reforma Hotel though many newer ones had been built in the outer residential quarters. The uniformed doorman greeted the Señora with deference and the manager came out from his office to assure her the usual rooms were at her disposal, the high-ceilinged corner bedroom and sitting room overlooking a side street away from the clanging traffic of the main avenue.

The Señora had slept in the car, but she undressed and lay down again as Conchita moved to and fro about the rooms, setting everything in order, dresses hung in the closet, linen laid in the drawers, her toilet things, the tortoise-shell brushes and silver-topped bottles, arranged on the dressing table.

"Enough, Conchita. I expect the Señora Pérez at five. Tell them outside we will want tea, a good tea, toast and cakes."

Yes, she thought to herself, her old friend was a greedy old woman, too fat, but she would be full of news, full as the cakes with currants, and the Señora looked forward to an hour of gentle gossip. Not so many friends left here in the city. Once society had been as elegant as any in Europe. Now it was gaudy, restless, the old families gone, the younger men and women rushing about in fast cars, hopping into planes, grabbing at each other's husbands and wives, dashing in and out, building hideous concrete houses full of bright glitter. Much talk of money made too easily, lost and remade again. No wonder that, under it all, crime festered in the streets, new crimes, kidnaping, rape, and robbery. Crime had always existed in Mexico but of a different sort. She remembered when bandits lurked on the old highways. Her husband, always, went armed as they drove out into the country, but crime now crept everywhere, and she thought again of the man left on the priest's doorstep.

The telephone rang announcing Señora Pérez. A short stout woman in traditional Spanish black came in, chains rattling as she greeted the Señora. *"Cuanto gusto,* Sara, so long since I have seen you." She settled herself in an armchair, her two feet placed carefully together. The tea was brought. Between mouthfuls of sweet cake Señora Pérez chattered comfortably, retailing news of her family, then going on to speak of mutual friends, describing marriages, births, old and new scandals, dwelling on the last with considerable relish.

Señora Martínez said little, for much of this seemed unimportant echoes from another life. She sat wondering why she had bothered with María Pérez, but her attention was suddenly caught by the mention of José Mendes as Señora Pérez leaned forward, her diamond-ringed fingers reaching for another cake.

"You remember José, Sara, Miguel's younger brother. He's made millions. No one knows how, has built himself a fine new house and a big villa in Acapulco, entertains the queerest people, gamblers, movie stars, and worse. There's a lot of talk about him." Señora Pérez lowered her voice. "Some say he's mixed up in very shady business, arms, even drugs. Terrible for Miguel. A good thing his old mother is not alive."

Picturing that lady, a fierce matriarch who had frightened her as a bride, Señora Martínez agreed she would hardly have approved her son's conduct, though privately she might have taken malicious satisfaction in his material success. Most of the Pérez men had been dull fellows.

The last tidbits of news and the last cakes disposed of, Señora Pérez rose almost reluctantly, her chains clattering again as she reached up to kiss Señora Martínez.

"Such a pleasure, so good to have seen you," then, wistfully, "Too few of us left . . ." Looking back as she went through the door, she turned. "You do not change, Sara, it was good, very good of you to let me come."

Poor María, never very bright, but Señora Martínez was

glad if the visit had given her any pleasure. She'd scarcely listened to her old friend's chatter, but she was sorry for the Mendes family, sorry to hear José had joined too many others in this new world of glare and shadow. One reason his name had caught her attention, not long ago he'd been reported visiting in Cuernavaca. None of her friends had seen him, though that meant nothing if he now moved in other circles.

Dismissing him from her thoughts, she turned her mind to the evening before her. She liked the American Ambassador, a good, hard-working man, a bachelor, whose pleasant manners and sympathetic understanding of Mexican problems made him popular in a difficult post. The dinner for a group of visiting American senators should be interesting, and she was curious to see what Mexican officials would be there. The Foreign Minister, of course, and some others. One or two she might know but there were new faces in the government this year.

Conchita had laid out the lace dress and drawn her bath. Afterwards the Señora came in to sit while the maid brushed her hair, arranged it in its high pompadour, and set a jeweled comb at the back. Carefully the Señora stepped into the dress and sat down again to fix the great diamond earrings that swung as she moved to put on rings and bracelets. She rose and stood before the mirror.

"There, Conchita, are you satisfied?"

Conchita looked grim approval as if congratulating herself on her mistress's appearance. She took down a silk wrap and put it over the Señora's shoulders, handed her a gold evening purse, and went with her down the hall.

Ector was waiting at the hotel door and they drove out the brightly lit avenue through the residential quarter, handsome houses set side by side behind walls or flowered lawns. The American Embassy was an imposing structure, square and

solid, looming above wrought-iron gates that opened as the
car approached. A short circular drive led to the main entrance, where a uniformed doorman ushered the Señora up
shallow steps into a wide vestibule. Here a young attaché
waited to escort her to the drawing room.

The Ambassador came forward at once, greeting her cordially.

"I do appreciate your coming. I had given up hope of
enticing you from Cuernavaca." He turned to a tall gray-
haired man. "Senator Thomas, let me present you to a distinguished compatriot, Señora Martínez. The Señora comes
too rarely to the embassy. We are especially fortunate to
have her with us this evening, a tribute, I'm sure, to you and
your colleagues."

The Chairman of the Senate Foreign Relations Committee
bowed over the Señora's hand.

"A great pleasure to meet you, Señora. I've heard much
about you from mutual friends in Washington."

They chatted for a moment, interrupted by a short black-
mustachioed man, Señor Cárdenas, the Foreign Minister, his
importance emphasized by the string of medals on his coat
lapel and the broad colored ribbon spanning his stout chest.

"Señora. An unexpected honor. We have missed you here
in the City."

Others of the guests gathered about the Señora as she made
polite response to the Minister and spoke with the few old
friends among the company. Those she did not know were
duly introduced by Henry Cooper, who had come to stand
alongside her. The Señora was glad to see the young man and
amused by his whispered comments on the various personal-
ities present.

"You've met Senator Thomas. The small fellow with the
red face is Senator Harper, regular firebrand. The thin one

with the Lincoln look, Senator Crowder from Nebraska, very long on corn and crops, the hawk-eyed younger man, Haskins, suspicious type on the lookout for Communists in the bushes. That's Morado, the new Minister of Justice, just coming through the door. I believe you're sitting next him, Senator Thomas on your other side. You've not met the Minister? I'll bring him across."

Henry came back with a short, broad-shouldered man, stiff black hair cut en brosse over a high-cheekboned face dark enough to hint at Indian blood. Henry made the presentation and turned as a stout, bespangled dowager fell upon the Señora with glad cries.

"*Querida*, what happiness to see you, Sara." The dark man stood by as Señora Martínez introduced "His Excellency the Minister of Justice," at whom the stout lady gave a startled look and scuttled off to more familiar territory. The Minister smiled and offered his arm to the Señora as the procession, led by the Ambassador and the wife of the Foreign Minister, made its way toward the dining room.

"As you see, señora, I'm not too popular in some circles. I'm sorry if I frightened your poor friend."

"Justice, true justice, is often frightening, Excellency."

The Minister gave his partner a sharp look as they went around the table and found their places. He had heard about this lady, an American, the widow of a distinguished Mexican diplomat. He knew she lived in Cuernavaca, somewhat of a recluse but respected by all who knew her.

Señora Martínez glanced around the table, the usual diplomatic dinner, reminding her of so many she had given, so many she had attended in so many places, the women in their jewels and brocades, the men, some important, some self-important, two or three pretty young girls flirting with young secretaries, ornaments as necessary as flowers in the centerpiece. It was all familiar but she was enjoying herself, and, as the Senator turned, talking of news of Washington friends, they chatted pleasantly enough. Course followed course, the traditional soup, fish, meat, salad and dessert. The Ambassador, she noted, had a good chef.

The Señora sensed her neighbor on the right found his partner, a brittle-voiced young woman, rather hard going. She turned to include him in a mild political discussion she was having with the Senator. To her surprise the Mexican was very knowledgeable about American affairs, speaking in a quiet way, listening carefully to all that was said. Later, when the Senator's attention was taken by the wife of the Foreign Minister on his other side, she asked Señor Morado if he had lived much in the United States.

"When I left the university here I studied law at Berkeley in California, then took a job with the Police Department in Los Angeles. They needed a liaison man to handle Mexican problems."

"But that is most interesting. And now . . . ?"

"I returned some few years ago, practiced law here until this new government came in and appointed me to my present post."

"A very responsible one and very full of problems, I imagine."

"Human nature is much the same in any country, in any city, señora, but the problems today are new ones. Drugs in particular. This is my real worry. Money can be made too quickly and frontiers scarcely exist for the planes that fly back and forth every day. We do our best but the trouble is widespread, both in your country and in mine, indeed in all the world. Small men, as well as big men, are easily corrupted. The gains are enormous and so the traffic goes on. Even your town of Cuernavaca may not be immune."

"That is true. I live very retired, but I read the papers. As for Cuernavaca, once it was a sleepy old city; now we have a large mixed population of a hundred thousand. Inevitably we have our share of crime."

"You are fortunate, señora, to be away from it all."

There was a pause as the Ambassador rose to propose a toast to his visiting guests to which Senator Thomas made a graceful response. The dinner ended as further toasts were exchanged to the President of Mexico and the President of the United States. As the company returned to the drawing room, the Minister of Justice bowed and kissed the Señora's hand.

"It has been a privilege to have met you, señora. I have already made my excuses to the Ambassador and I regret that I must bid you good evening. We keep late hours in my office. As you said, justice can be a hard taskmaster."

Señora Martínez looked after the man as, without further good-bys, he slipped quietly out into the hall. A new brand of Mexican official, one that roused her interest and curiosity. She wondered at his reference to Cuernavaca, natural perhaps, but could he have known of the murder in her street? No, that small sordid crime could not have any connection with the bigger evils of which he spoke.

The party broke up. The Ambassador escorted the Señora to the door where they chatted for a moment. Thanking him for a delightful evening, she remarked, "You are lucky in your staff. I've seen something of that nice young man Henry Cooper."

"I'm glad you like him, a very fine officer, came to us with a splendid record. Unfortunately he's soon due for transfer. Washington has its eye on him."

"A pity he's leaving. I introduced him to a charming girl the other day. They seemed much taken with each other."

The Ambassador laughed. "You ladies are incorrigible matchmakers."

"Perhaps, but my efforts on your behalf seem to have failed miserably."

"I'm afraid mine is a lost cause."

The Señora shook her head, bade him good-by, and got into her car.

Back in the hotel Conchita was waiting for her mistress. Though tired, the Señora had enjoyed her evening. Everyone had been very kind. Her old friends had urged her to stay longer, but instinct told her she must return to Cuernavaca, so she instructed Conchita to have Ector ready at ten next morning.

It was good to get into bed. Only then did she admit to herself, "One grows old."


On the Monday morning Pepe had weeded the garden beds, skimmed the swimming pool of leaves, swept the patio and the graveled paths, all the while thinking of what he would say to Father Rodríguez. Later, his work finished, he went into the kitchen, where he shared lunch with Marta. The kitchen was a friendly place without Conchita's disapproving eye, and it was a good lunch, a big bowl of beans and fresh tortillas, topped off with the red finger bananas from the tree outside. The woman and the boy chatted together and Pepe felt more cheerful as he gathered up his schoolbooks and walked through the back gate to knock at Father Rodríguez's door. The old brown Indian woman who looked after the Father let him into the little study where the priest sat writing at his desk. Pepe laid down his books, began to speak, then hesitated.

The priest looked up at the boy. "What's on your mind, Pepe?"

Words came slowly, fearfully. "The man on the street, the man who was killed. I saw his face. It . . . it was like a man I'd seen before."

"What are you trying to tell me, Pepe?"

"That man, I think he was one of the workmen at the Doctor's place. I saw him last time I went home, last month. He was drinking with other men outside the cafe."

"And you believe it was the same man?"

"I am sure, very sure. He didn't belong in the village, that's why I noticed him."

"Have you told anyone else about this?"

"I was frightened. At first I wasn't sure, but now . . . They say there was a fight up there. One of the new men, one of a lot that came in from Puebla, ran off, so I thought, if he was the man I'd seen . . ."

"Who is 'they,' Pepe?"

"A—a friend of mine who'd been to the village on Saturday, and yesterday at my aunt's, she said there'd been more trouble at the Doctor's. Some of the men who work there, men from our own village, are very bad."

"Did you hear the man's name, the man who ran away?"

"Pablo, my friend said."

The priest had listened carefully to Pepe's story. Now he got up and put his hand on the boy's shoulder.

"Don't worry, Pepe. You did very right to come to me. I will talk to the police captain. What you have told me may be of great help. And now to our lessons."

After he told his story to the priest, Pepe's mind was more at ease. Sitting down at the desk, he sorted out his books and the man and the boy were soon hard at work. Light came in through the half-open shutters, long shafts of sunlight spilling over the desk where Pepe carefully filled pages of lined paper as Father Rodríguez dictated the English words.

Later came the history lesson, Mexican history today. Pepe listened as the priest told of the Mayans and the Aztecs, of the great pyramids, temples, and palaces they had built and the vast hordes of treasure accumulated, gold and jade and curious carvings, feathered cloaks and headdresses. He told of the coming of the Spaniards, how the Great King welcomed them, believing the white men to be angel beings from another world, and of the fine presents he gave to Cortes, the leader. Before too long, however, the Great King was killed, his people enslaved, the treasures looted by Cortes and his Spaniards and the soldiers and the priests who came after him to rule the country. Not all of them were bad or greedy, many were good men and later others, hundreds, thousands even, came to settle, to build towns and churchs, to plant crops and cultivate the fields. "As time went on there were troubled years of war and revolution, a nation grows slowly, but remember, Pepe, any Mexican, whether of Spanish or Indian descent, should be proud of his forebears. We should be happy to live in this land they made together."

This was solemn talk, but Pepe listened attentively. He'd seen pictures of the Spanish horsemen in armor, helmets on their heads. He'd seen pictures of the Great King Montezuma in his colored robes. He wondered what had become of the treasures.

"Did the Spaniards take all of the gold, Padre?"

"No, not all of it. Much was hidden away, buried. Some has been dug up and is in museums or in private collections. More may be in the ground, not only gold but statues, big and small. Anything that is found now must be turned over to the state, for it belongs here in Mexico and cannot be sold or taken away."

"The Doctor, is he looking for gold?"

"That and other things. He believes that some of Cortes's treasure may be buried near your village close to the old Taxco road. So far nothing much has turned up, but he keeps trying."

Pepe looked at the priest, then down again to his paper. He wondered if he should tell Father Rodríguez what his aunt had said about the man Pedro. His aunt talked a lot. It might make trouble, more trouble for the people in the village. Before he could say anything there was a knock at the front door. The old Indian woman padded down the hall, then came to the study.

"A señor asking for the Padre."

Father Rodríguez got up. "Enough for this afternoon, Pepe." He took down a book from a high shelf, handed it to the boy.

"A story you might like. Read it and you will understand more of what we talked of today."

The book was calf bound with a gold crest stamped on its cover, the leather smooth and worn. Pepe put it carefully with his others, said a polite *"Buenas tardes"* to the Father, and went out down the back path to the Casa Santa Luiza's garden gate.

As he stepped into his office on Tuesday morning, Henry Cooper's telephone rang. The Ambassador had already come in and would like to see Mr. Cooper at once. Hoping no senator had been robbed or waylaid in a night club the evening before, Henry reflected they were a sober lot and nothing worse could have happened than a sudden attack of indigestion after the embassy chef's excellent dinner. He hurried down the hall, however, and the Ambassador's secretary ushered him into the inner office, where his distinguished chief sat at his mahogany desk flanked by the American and State Department flags.

Motioning Henry to a seat, the Ambassador laid a sheaf of cables down before him.

"These have just come in, high priority, 'Eyes Only,' but they're down your alley, I believe."

Lately a good share of Henry's work had been concerned with the growing drug traffic between Mexico and the United States. Though it was not strictly a CIA affair, he had been assigned to make certain investigations by the agency, investigations that might reveal tie-ups with subversive guerrilla groups here and in other Latin American countries. Money from drugs ran into large figures which could well be used to buy men and arms. So far the Mexican Government, and the Minister of Justice in particular, had shown ready co-operation, but the traffic grew daily and scant progress had been made in spotting the sources or the men who controlled them. Not long ago the Ambassador had asked Henry to make a report in depth on the situation. This had received favorable notice in Washington and new instructions had come in, the cables which Henry was now reading.

"A very nasty business."

"I agree, sir. Stop one leak and a dozen more turn up; cut off one head and a dozen more are there smiling at you."

"Hopeless, you think?"

"It would seem so. There's been progress on the French end, not so much shipped in from Marseilles, but the Far East traffic makes up for that."

"And here?"

"Bad as ever. The government is playing ball, but once they clear acres of planted stuff the farmers replant next week."

"I suppose it's the big boys we should be looking for, the men behind the racket."

"Easier said than done, sir. We have a list of names a mile long. Might as well use the Mexican Who's Who, but we can't pin anyone down."

"You met Morado, the new Minister of Justice, last night."

"Yes, a very good man and anxious to do his part. He's set up a task force to get things on the road."

"You've talked with him?"

"Not yet. I've seen his deputy, who promised me an appointment."

"I'll call Morado myself, let him know I've asked you to handle our end of the business."

"I thought I had one small lead. Matter of fact that's why I requested Friday morning off. Señora Martínez had asked me for lunch and that gave me a chance to look around. I'd heard there might be a fellow in Cuernavaca worth watching, but he'd gone when I got there, Luis Gómez, a big swell who vacations in Acapulco."

"I gathered from the Señora you managed to mix business with pleasure on Friday."

The young man smiled. "The Señora was right, sir. I went back on Sunday, strictly on pleasure that time."

"Good for you. The Señora says she's very attractive. I hope your investigation proceeds smoothly. Guess that's all for now, Henry. I'll get on to the Justice Ministry at once."


Dr. Hartung was a painstaking if not a brilliant scholar. His early reputation had been made in Greece, where he had been lucky enough to unearth a dramatic find of Mycenaean relics. Returning to his native Norway, he was elected to the chair of archaeology at the Royal University. He was a facile speaker and much in demand as lecturer, and he traveled widely. A chance meeting with experts from the Mexico City museum aroused his curiosity about pre-Columbian civilization and, after considerable study and correspondence with the state authorities, he persuaded himself there were still opportunities for discovery in the Taxco area. Reluctant permission was given for a small expedition, and the good professor and his wife had come to Cuernavaca and settled themselves within easy distance of the proposed dig.

An agreeable couple, they soon made friends. Everyone was sympathetic though unimpressed by the collection of broken pots and old bits of metal so far accumulated. The finds seemed more likely to have come from Cortes's kitchen refuse than his treasury. Lately there had been trouble at the dig. The expedition was shorthanded. A young Norwegian assistant had been taken ill and the Doctor was obliged to rely on the help of his wife, who sorted and catalogued his finds, depending on local labor for the actual work on the site. He paid good wages, and at first the men had seemed willing enough to follow his instructions, but lately they had grown surly and spent more time in the village cafe than at work. The foreman, Pedro, when spoken to, was actually insolent.

In spite of all this the Doctor refused to be discouraged, and just last week, prospecting on his own, he had discovered what he thought might be the entrance to an underground cave. It was late in the afternoon. Calling to one of the men, he told him to dig out the hole, cover it carefully, and say nothing to any of the others. The man seemed to understand, but when the Doctor returned next day there appeared to be no trace of work done and the man was not to be found. Questioning the foreman brought no satisfaction beyond a shrug of the shoulders, "He was a bad lot, collected his money and ran off." As the cave seemed undisturbed, the

Doctor kept its discovery to himself, resolving to make his own investigation, but he was sufficiently excited to confide in Father Rodríguez, and it was of this they had talked when they lunched at the Señora's.

Mrs. Hartung had left Friday afternoon to visit friends in Taxco, where her husband would join her early in the week. Setting off alone on Tuesday morning the Doctor determined to stop at the dig site en route. Timing his arrival for noon when the men would be eating and drinking in the cafe, he parked his car by the gate. There was no sign of the old watchman, so he took out his own key, unlocked the gate, and walked up the hill. Glad of the chance to be unobserved, he gathered up pick and shovel and a flashlight from one of the huts and went down through the brush on the far side. He had to search for several minutes among the rocks and mesquite. A lizard ran across his feet, and, overhead, there was the whine of a plane scudding across the sky. Finally, at the bottom of a shallow gully, he came on the hole partly concealed by branches laid over the entrance. Putting his tools aside, the Doctor got down on his knees, flashlight in hand, shoved the branches away, and peered into the hole. A cave, right enough, and a large one.

Dr. Hartung crawled forward. There was no room to stand inside the cave, but the floor seemed to have been swept clean of rocks and dirt. Over in a corner the flash showed a pile of small boxes, neatly stacked cardboard cartons. He reached out, took hold of one. It was curiously light. He turned it over, found it carefully sealed and numbered. These were obviously new boxes and, to the Doctor's disappointment, could have nothing to do with buried treasure. But what did they contain and how and why were they hidden here in the cave? Looking around for anything that might tell him or give any hint, he noticed a few cigarette butts, one of which he put in his pocket. Farther on the light shone on a broken bottle, nothing else, only a sprinkling of white powder which sifted onto the floor as he lifted still another box from the pile.

Flashing his light around the walls, high up, at the very back of the cave, he made out a small aperture between the rocks. Could this be an opening into another cave? If so, it had not been disturbed. There was a heap of stones at the base which might have been used to close the entrance. Impossible to reach the crack above with his flashlight and equally impossible to move the rocks away without tools. Nothing more to be done for the moment. There remained the mystery of the boxes. Should he leave them alone or take one out with him? He crawled back to examine them once more. A sudden wild suggestion crossed his mind and he scraped up grains of the white powder from the floor, twisting them into his handkerchief. Slowly he made his way out of the hole, through the brush, and up the bank. From the other side came the sound of voices. The men had come back. Carefully edging around out of sight, the Doctor reached the church, pushed through the door, sat down on one of the benches, and brushed the dirt from his clothes. He sat for some minutes, trying to make sense of what he had found in the cave. Certainly the dig workers must be questioned, but they were a rough lot and he had little hope of getting satisfactory answers. Better, perhaps, to say nothing until he could inform the local authorities. That would be the easiest way, of course, but no, he must speak to the foreman, Pedro. Shaking himself, he got up, opened the door, and walked across to the men gathered around the dig.

"*Buenos días.* Found anything this morning?"

One of them turned aside, spat on his spade. Another

laughed, held up a rusted spoon. "Only this." He tossed it into the dirt.

"Where is Pedro?"

"Over there, by the hut."

Dr. Hartung walked up to the tool shed, where the big man sat lounging on a broken chair. As the Doctor came toward him, he rose slowly to his feet.

"Sorry we've found so little here. I came along this morning to look over the ground. What do you know about a cave on the other side?"

The man's eyes flickered. "Never saw it."

"There's a good-sized opening that seems to have been recently dug out."

"Probably some animal's hole."

"No, someone has been down there. I want to know who they were and what they were doing."

Pedro shrugged his shoulders.

"I've seen no one."

"I don't believe you." The Doctor turned, calling to one of the men by the dig. "Tell me. There's a hole down below. Any of you been working there?"

The man looked at Pedro, shook his head. The others stood silent.

"That fellow who ran away," Pedro blustered, "he was always pottering about, going off on his own."

"You think he was the one who dug out the cave entrance? That was an important discovery. You still say none of you knew about it?"

"Look here, old man," the voice was truculent, "the fellow was no good. He made trouble, we were glad to get rid of him."

"And the cave, did any of you look inside?"

There were murmurs among the men.

"Why should we? We've enough work here."

"I've looked inside and I didn't like what I saw. I'm notifying the police."

Pedro, head down, stepped forward. "We don't want the police here. Forget about the cave. It's nothing to do with you, none of your business." He was face to face with the Doctor now. "No police, you understand." Instinctively Dr. Hartung retreated as the foreman came closer, fists swinging. He looked behind him. The other men were standing well aside, no help there. Though not a timid man, the good Doctor had never encountered naked violence and Pedro looked like a great bear as he lunged toward him. The Doctor turned, started down the hill, but Pedro came after him, followed by two of the men. Running, he stumbled and fell. The three stood over him, Pedro shouting at the others left behind to keep their distance. There were a few seconds of loud talk and suddenly the Doctor felt himself grabbed. Pedro pulled him up by the arms and was dragging him toward the gate. Opening the door of the Doctor's car, they bundled him inside. Pedro and one of the men got into the front. The third kept tight hold of the Doctor in the back. The poor man spluttered helplessly, tried to look out as Pedro started the car and turned it around, but the old gatekeeper was not there. The gears meshed hard as Pedro swung the car off down the road.

Badly frightened now and half stunned, Dr. Hartung tried to speak, but his companion cuffed him roughly across the mouth. Cowering in his corner, he could only wait, wondering what the brutes would do next, kill him perhaps and pitch him out on the road. Pedro drove fast, bypassed the village onto the main highway. Almost unconscious, the Doctor hardly noticed when they turned off again and finally stopped before a huddle of buildings. Pedro got out, leaving the others on guard. They were in a kind of deserted farmyard. It was quiet except for some chickens that went clucking about. A brown cur dog came to sniff at the car until one of the men kicked him away. Pedro returned, ordered the men to take the Doctor out of the car, throwing something, a blanket, over his head. Pedro led the way across the yard behind one of the buildings to where a wooden door swung open above a short flight of stone steps. Down they went into a dark underground tunnel which came out into a high-roofed room, empty and damp, the only light from a grille high up on one side. Dumping the Doctor in a corner, Pedro reached down to feel his pockets and pulled out the flash.

"You won't need that here."

He handed it to one of the men.

"Hold this while I tie him up." Taking the scarf from his neck, he knotted it tightly round the Doctor's hands, then tossed the blanket onto the floor.

"Keep yourself warm, old man. May be a long wait before the police come."

The Doctor lay still as the men left, their laughter echoing as they went out down the tunnel.


The two men who called on Father Rodríguez Monday afternoon were police officers. The man murdered on Friday still lay unidentified in the morgue and they had come to question the priest again. This time Father Rodríguez had information which he knew must be given to the police. Anxious to protect the boy Pepe, he listened carefully, thinking how best to compose his answers.

The dead man was obviously a laborer. Laboratory tests of dust and dirt from his clothing and hands confirmed this. He had been repeatedly stabbed and died, probably within minutes of his discovery by the passing postman. Not much sign of struggle, must have been taken unawares by his assailant. Could the Padre give any explication for his being found on his doorstep?

"You know, señores, many people come to me, many strangers, people I do not even know. Whenever possible I am glad to help them. This man may have been one of those. I did not recognize him. Afterwards I have thought he reminded me of a worker employed at Dr. Hartung's archaeological dig on the Taxco road. I am not at all sure, but it might be well to make inquiries. I have heard there has been trouble there among the crew and, after a fight a man, Pablo by name, ran off some days ago. This man and two others came recently from Puebla; the rest were recruited from the village near the dig."

The policemen exchanged looks, one nodded as if in agreement.

"Dr. Hartung was here on Friday. Did he see the body before it was removed?"

"No. Dr. and Mrs. Hartung came later to lunch with Señora Martínez next door. At the time there was no reason to suspect the victim was one of his men."

Taking a small object from his brief case, the police captain unwrapped it and laid it on the priest's desk.

Father Rodríguez bent to examine it. "A Spanish gold coin!"

"We found this sewn in one of the dead man's pockets. What you have just told us might well mean it came from the dig."

"If that is so Dr. Hartung will be delighted. So far very little of value has turned up."

Father Rodríguez took the coin in his hand, turned it over. "The Cortes period. Genuine, no doubt about it. My father had one like it, carried it as a pocket piece." Almost reluctantly he gave it over to the police captain. The latter wrapped the coin again and put it back into his brief case, folded up his notebook, signaled to his companion, and the two officers started toward the door.

"If the Doctor can identify the man for us, so much the better. We have his address and will get on to him at once." He paused. "You yourself, Padre, would you be willing to view the body?"

"I'm at your disposal, señores, but my recollection is too uncertain to be of much use."

"In any event we are grateful for your help, and will keep you informed as soon as we have talked with the Doctor."

The priest ushered his visitors out, returned to his study, and sat down again at the desk, his mind full of thoughtful surmises. Happily he had been able to keep Pepe's name out of the discussion. He'd no wish to involve the boy in what might turn out to be a dirty business. If Dr. Hartung identified the man as Pablo, well and good. Let the police take care of the rest. It might prove to be no more than the result of a quarrel among the dig workers. Still, that hardly explained the man's coming to him, if indeed that had been his intention. But that too might be cleared up in some ordinary way. As for the Spanish coin, that was another matter and, if actually found at the dig, could have real significance for the Doctor and his work.

The old Indian woman shuffled in with a tray. Tea and biscuits, a habit he had learned in the student years he spent in England. For tea and biscuits, and for those happy, carefree years he was very grateful.

Arrived at the Ministry of Justice, Henry Cooper showed his card to the policeman on duty at the gate and was duly escorted upstairs and down long corridors to an outer office where an efficient young woman took his name and entered it in the book before her.

"The Minister expects you, señor, but he is engaged at the moment. Please, will you take a seat?"

Henry chose a chair opposite and looked out the window. The pollution was not bad today and the sun shone brightly on the packed traffic rushing to and fro across the square. Sirens and horns screamed from below, the usual morning chaos as cars came pushing through from intersections that fed into the main avenue. No wonder pedestrian subways had been dug throughout the city center. Crossings could not be controlled and accidents were frequent. But traffic problems were not his concern, so he gave his attention to the matters to be laid before the Minister.

A telephone rang on the secretary's desk.

"Señor Morado is free now." Ushering him toward a door on the far side, she opened it. "Señor Cooper, Excelensia."

From behind his desk the Minister came forward.

"Good morning, Mr. Cooper. Your ambassador tells me we have matters to discuss. Won't you sit down?"

"Very kind of you to receive me so promptly, sir."

The Minister smiled. "We Mexicans have a reputation for '*mañana*,' putting off things too long. My American training taught me otherwise. Shall we get to our business?"

Henry took papers from his brief case and proceeded to detail his instructions from Washington. The Minister listened carefully, now and then making notes on a pad. This man was impressive, thought Henry, and certainly a new type of Mexican official. He asked pertinent questions and soon the two men were deep in the affairs of the moment.

"You understand, Mr. Cooper, we are disposed to give you every possible co-operation. Our resources are not as large as they should be, and I am sorry to say the public is apathetic. So far our own people have not been too seriously affected by the drug problem, but it is the increasing traffic going abroad that disturbs us, that and the drugs brought into Mexico and channeled from here into the United States. For some years marijuana has been exported, but I understand that is even grown in American back yards today. Still, large shipments go out and profits to Mexican farmers are high. An alarming new factor is the quantity of cocaine coming in from Chile, for example. This is a serious matter and steps must be taken to stop it. We do what we can but it is very difficult. Persons in high places are involved, protection is easily bought and one must tread carefully."

"All this we understand, Mr. Minister."

"If we could ever strike at one or more of the men responsible, the directing heads, then others might take fright, but these men are well hidden behind walls of privilege and wealth. We have many names"—he threw his hands wide—"how to reach them? If you can help us, so much the better."

"You have been very frank, Mr. Minister, and I can assure you my own government appreciates your difficulties. As you know criminal justice encounters similar obstacles in the United States. There are agencies at work to thwart our investigations, the police themselves are often involved, but if I can serve you here in any way the Ambassador has authorized me to do so."

The Minister reached for a cigarette from a box on the desk.

"I have heard, Mr. Cooper, that you already have suspicions concerning one individual."

"Suspicions, sir, but no evidence."

"I realize that. The man in question belongs to one of our

oldest families, a playboy, like some others, but one who may not have confined himself to harmless play. José Mendes. Lately he has associated himself with dubious characters here in the city, in Cuernavaca and in Acapulco, where he has a big house and lives in elaborate style. We have reason to believe he has a finger in many odd activities, not only drugs but smuggling of all sorts, even the illegal export of antiquities. The drug business is of course the most important, but there is a great vogue for pre-Columbian art in the United States and Europe. Large prices are paid by collectors and museums and no questions asked. So much for Señor Mendes. If you could bring us information on this one man or his confederates, real information, we could proceed against him. His arrest and conviction would bring wide publicity and we would have made a fine start.

"My assistant, Mr. García, has already done some work on the Mendes case. I will ask him to show you anything he has. García, by the way, has my complete confidence and I will tell him to give you any necessary support."

Taking up the telephone, the Minister said a few words in rapid Spanish, then rose to shake hands with his visitor.

"The best of luck, Mr. Cooper. My secretary will take you to García's office."

The assistant García proved to be a young man, slim, keen eyed, speaking fair English but obviously pleased by Henry's fluent Spanish. The two men went to work at once, Henry reading over the papers in the Mendes dossier, asking questions and checking his own information with that already reported.

"This Cuernavaca angle, what do you make of it?"

"It's possible there is a Mendes correspondent there, probably an important one, so far unidentified. You know about the murder in the Calle Costanza?" García asked.

"I do indeed. It happened last Friday shortly before I arrived to lunch with Señora Martínez at the Casa Santa Luiza. The man was discovered in front of the priest's house next door."

"It may have been an ordinary occurrence, but the police are not satisfied. No one has come forward to claim the body and just this morning they reported a curious discovery, an old Spanish coin sewn in a pocket of the man's clothes. Señor Morado has told you of Mendes' possible commerce in antiques. The coin is not of great value, but it might well have been picked up by the dead man from a bigger haul."

"At the Señora's I met a Norwegian archaeologist, Dr. Hartung. He has a dig on the Taxco road, not a very productive one, I'm afraid. It seems unlikely real treasure could have been discovered there, otherwise it would be known. Dr. Hartung is an enthusiastic man and would certainly have mentioned any big find."

"Perhaps. In any event no lead is too small for us to follow. Could you find some reason to go to Cuernavaca again? Find what you can there, then, if you think best, go on to Acapulco. It might be useful for you to make contact with Mendes himself, easier for an American than for any of us. He keeps open house, entertains on a grand scale. Coming from the embassy, you shouldn't have any trouble. I will arrange for one of our men, Ramón Verdes, to keep in touch with you in Cuernavaca and Acapulco. You'll find him useful, he knows both towns well. Let us know where you will be staying."

"You realize, García, this is a fishing expedition. I can't promise too much."

"Anything you bring back may be of help. We can only hope the fish will bite, even a small catch will be welcome."

The two men shook hands. Henry went out. The noon traffic was very thick in the square. Hailing a passing taxi, one of those that cruised up and down the main avenues depositing passengers at any required corner, he wedged himself between two fat men as the driver plunged ahead, sounding his horn and threading his way around cars and buses.

Some distance down the Reforma, Henry rapped on the window, stumbled over his companion's feet, and got out to walk the rest of the way to the embassy. Time enough, he thought, to catch the Ambassador before he went home to lunch. Meanwhile it was good to be out in the air with a chance to consider the results of his conversations.

The Ambassador received him at once.

"Don't tell me too much, Henry. Unlike some of his colleagues Morado's a man I trust. Take as much time off as you need. I'll back you up here. Get on with the job. Whatever comes out of it is to our mutual benefit."

Returning to his own office, Henry arranged to cancel various appointments and social engagements. "I'll be out of town for a few days doing a bit of overdue sightseeing," he mentioned to one of the younger secretaries he met in the corridor.

"Better try Acapulco if you get tired of pyramids and churches."

"I might do that. Not much fun going there alone, however."

"Latch onto José Mendes, always something going on at his house, and plenty of girls to go round."

"Do you know the man?"

"Jean Bertrand from the French Embassy took me there last month. We had a roaring evening. Tell Mendes I told you about it. He'll be delighted, has a glad hand out for anybody."

Tony Farrar was not one of the embassy's brightest stars,

more adept at social affairs than diplomatic correspondence, but Henry thanked him for his advice, so unexpectedly useful.

"If I get to Acapulco, I'll send you a naughty postcard with a list of good addresses."

The other laughed. "I collected a few of those myself."

In his office again Henry put in a call to Arabella's boutique. Long-distance calls in Mexico can be difficult—much chatter between operators, strange buzzes and whines on the line, then complete silence. Another try. Success this time, but it was Mrs. Harvey who answered.

"How nice to hear from you, Mr. Cooper. Are you coming to Cuernavaca soon again? The weather is perfect here. You want Arabella? She's busy just now with a customer. Will you hold on?"

More whines and buzzes, but finally Arabella's voice, faint but her own.

"Can you hear me? It's Henry. I've business in Cuernavaca tomorrow. What about dinner? I'll call for you at the boutique, six, six-thirty. Don't say no. I'll be there."

He rang off, gathered up some papers from his desk, and hurried out. He would need money, so he stopped at the bank, picked up clothes from the cleaners, ordered his car serviced at the garage, and went back to his apartment to prepare for an early start next morning.


At lunch in the Casa Santa Luiza kitchen on Tuesday, Conchita was full of the visit to Mexico City. The Señora had looked like a queen as she went off to the embassy. She was tired, yes, but she had enjoyed herself. She, Conchita, had met an old friend that evening. They had dined at a restaurant and gone out to walk on the boulevard. The lights, the people, the shops, Conchita's eyes glistened as she retailed every incident to Marta, who rattled her pans and said Cuernavaca was good enough for her.

In her room beside the patio Señora Martínez rested through the long afternoon, then got up to walk in the garden. The flowers had been newly watered. She stooped over the roses, raising their heads after the heat of the day. She had asked Father Rodríguez to take supper with her. Pepe brought them drinks as they sat together on the patio terrace. Above the walls the sun set behind the blue mountains as they grew purple against the dying fire in the sky. They talked of her evening at the embassy, of her conversation with the Minister of Justice.

The priest agreed: "Yes, we need new blood, new, younger, men to face today's problems. We should be grateful we have at last a stable government. Mexico has seen enough wars and revolutions and we are lucky to escape the disorders suffered by some of our neighbors to the south."

"The Minister seemed very concerned about the drug traffic and the growing crime statistics here at home. He even indicated Cuernavaca might have its own troubles."

"In light of Friday's tragedy that may be so."

"But Carlos, you can't think that poor man on the sidewalk was connected with sinister plots. From all accounts he seemed such an ordinary fellow."

"How do we know, señora? Evil is no respecter of persons."

The priest went on to tell her of the visit the police made to him on Monday afternoon. Always careful not to mention Pepe, he said there was reason to believe the dead man might have been a certain Pablo, one of Dr. Hartung's workers, and he described the coin found in the man's pocket.

"The police wanted Dr. Hartung's address. They hoped that he could identify the body, but I've heard nothing since. I tried to call his house this morning but there was no answer."

"I think he and his wife are away. I remember they planned to visit friends in Taxco. She was going up Friday after the lunch and he was to follow later. What a satisfaction for the Doctor if the gold coin was really taken from the dig. He has worked so hard up there without results. Who knows now what else may be found?"

Their drinks finished, the two went in to dinner. Sensing his hostess must be tired, Father Rodríguez left soon after coffee. Señora Martínez walked through the garden with him to the gate. It was cool now, the moon had come up, the sky silver and black, as she returned to the house, called Conchita, and went back into her room.

The moon shone through the window of Pepe's hut. The boy slept, turning on his cot now and then as if dreaming. Suddenly he was awakened by sounds from the street outside, usually quiet until dawn. There was a noise of cars, a clanking truck, then voices. Pepe sat up. His mind put more or less at ease by his confession to Father Rodríguez, he still worried about the dead man. Suppose the murderer had come back to strike again, even to attack the Padre. Now thoroughly alarmed, he opened the door of the hut. Though fainter, the voices seemed to come from across the way. Pepe ran down the garden path to the Casa's gate. Afraid to unlock it, he took hold of the lower limb of a tree that hung over the front wall and hoisted himself high enough to peer through the branches into the street.

A truck was parked opposite the Fat Man's house, behind it another car. No sign of anyone in the street. The truck looked empty, but as he watched closer Pepe thought he saw movement, someone standing in the shadow of the other car. There were lights coming through the shutters of the Fat Man's house and he could hear voices but the words were indistinct. Trembling, Pepe clung to the tree. Minutes, long minutes, passed. Suddenly the house door opened and two men stepped out into the bright moonlight. Pepe recognized the bigger man. It was Pedro, the foreman from the Hartung dig, the big bully from Pepe's own village. What was he doing here in the middle of the night? Why had he come to the Fat Man's house? Now, very frightened lest he look up and catch sight of him in the tree, Pepe pushed himself deeper into the branches, still watching as the two men got into the truck, motioning the other to follow in the car behind, and drove off down the street.

All was quiet again and the lights went out in the house opposite. Pepe thought of the neighbors, wondered if any of them had heard the noise, then he thought of Beppo. As he climbed down out of the tree, he remembered that Beppo slept at the far end of the garden, a sound sleeper too. Perhaps he could see him tomorrow to find out if he knew anything. Then again, should he go first to the Padre, tell him what he had seen, or should he say nothing?

Marta looked at Pepe as he came into the kitchen for his breakfast next morning. "Are you sick? Pale as a ghost and eyes like saucers. I'd best get a dose for you from the Señora."

"Please no, Marta." Manfully he swallowed his coffee, tried to eat, but tucked bits of bread into his pockets. He'd

feed them to the birds. They had no worries to take away
their appetites. He, Pepe, had too many.

Much had happened behind the closed shutters of the Fat
Man's house. Gómez, the Fat Man himself, a frightening
figure in his crimson brocaded dressing gown, had met Pedro
and his companion, gun in hand, angrily demanding what
they meant by waking him at this hour. The two men stam-
mered out the news of the Doctor's discovery of the cave, his
abduction and their leaving him in the store cellar of the Vista
del Rey, safe enough, they thought, as Señor Gómez owned
the place.

The fat man thundered at them. "Fools that you are,
blundering again. I told you to take care of that rat Pablo.
You let him get away to come here, spill his story to the
priest."

"But we caught him, señor."

"Caught him on the old man's doorstep. The place has
been crawling with police ever since. And now you've kidnaped the Doctor, stashed him away on my property. Why
didn't you kill him too and have done with it?"

The two men looked at each other.

"We thought of it."

"Even better if you'd killed yourselves!"

The men cringed. "Stupid, pigs of peasants." Gómez paced
up and down the room, gun still in hand, then turned on them.

"How did you come here?"

"In the truck, señor. Berto is waiting outside in the Doctor's
car."

"Waiting to be picked up by the police, I suppose. Get
out now at once, both of you. Go back and empty the cave,

take everything out, everything, you understand. Put the stuff in the truck and drive it to this address."

Scribbling on a piece of paper, he handed it to Pedro.

"Leave the Doctor's car in front of his house. You know where he lives?"

Dumbly Pedro nodded.

"Don't go back to the Vista. I'll take care of the Doctor. If you want to live get clear of the village, far away as you can go I'm through with you here." He tossed a roll of bills to Pedro. "Keep your mouths shut wherever you are." He brandished the revolver in front of them. "If you so much as squeak we'll find you. Now get out fast. You stink!"

Gómez stood behind the door as the men stumbled down the steps. He waited until he heard the truck and car start. Cursing, he turned back into the house, walked over to a phone, called a number, then another, and gave orders to be carried out the next day. Still muttering, he went up the stairs, put out the lights, peered into the street to make sure all was quiet, took off his dressing gown, and hoisted his big bulk into his great carved bed, the curses fainter as he slept.


Early on Wednesday morning a car, a black station wagon, drove into the farmyard behind the Vista del Rey. The sun was already warm and bright. Two men were unloading manure into a truck, kicking aside the chickens who pecked at their heels. The driver of the station wagon hailed them. "Give us a hand with these barrels at the back. Take it easy. They're heavy and the chief doesn't want his wine shaken up."

A man sitting beside the driver got out to unhitch the tail

gate as the two farmworkers put down their pitchforks and walked over to the car.

"*Madre de Dios*," shouted the station-wagon driver. "Don't bounce them or they'll spring a leak. Steady now." He got out and watched as the barrels were lifted into a wheeled farm cart. "Take them down into the first storeroom. Put them alongside the two we brought up last week. Wait, I'll come with you." The driver followed as the men trundled the cart across the yard to the wooden door leading down into the cellars of the main building. A heavy lock hung from its iron hasp. The two farmworkers stood by as the driver produced a key and swung open the door. He called back, "I forgot the flash, bring it along." The second man rummaged about the car's front seat, then came over to hand the driver the light. Both men followed as the farmhands eased the cart down the steps into the dark tunnel ahead.

"Far enough." The light shone into a large storeroom lined with wine bins, casks, and barrels stowed at the back.

"Set them down over there, next to that far lot. We have to check on the empties. It'll take us some time. Leave the cart here. We'll let you know when we've finished."

One of the farmworkers grumbled, "We can't hang around. The boss is waiting for that load of manure."

"Guess we can manage ourselves, then." The car driver handed him a couple of pesos. "Have a drink before you come back. We'll lock up when we're through."

Peering down the tunnel to make sure the men had left and were out the door, the driver turned back into the storeroom. Off to one side against the wall stood four or five empty barrels. Two or three were still wet from dregs, but one looked comparatively dry. Stuffing an old burlap bag into the bottom, he loaded it onto the cart.

"If he puts up a fight we'll take him out in the barrel."

Pulling a pack of cigarettes from his pocket, he handed one to the other man. "Better wait until we're sure the coast is clear." He reached up, took a bottle from a bin, and knocked off the top. "Gómez won't miss this one. Have a swig." Between them they finished the bottle and tossed it away in a corner.

"Now you go out, take a look, see if anyone's around before we start moving."

The second man came back. "No one but the chickens. Some women out of sight down by the washhouse."

"Good."

Pushing the cart along, the two men went out into the tunnel, past several more storerooms, then stopped.

"This should be the one."

The flashlight showed the huddled figure of Dr. Hartung crouched in the far corner. Startled, the Doctor looked up, then drew back into the corner.

The driver reached down, hauled him up, the blanket falling off around his feet.

"Not a word, old man. We've come to get you out of here."

"Who are you? Where are you taking me?"

"You'll soon find out."

The Doctor struggled feebly as the two men took hold of him. The second man looked at the driver, then over to the barrel.

"Don't think we'll need it. Not much fight left in him."

The Doctor, near collapse with fright and bewilderment, could only allow himself to be half carried out the door and down the tunnel, his weak protests smothered as the driver threw the blanket over him again and lifted him into the back of the station wagon.

Turning the car, they were off down the road, the two men

laughing and joking at the idea of the Doctor arriving at Gómez's hideout in a barrel.

"Lucky we didn't have to use it. No sense of humor in the fat bastard. Have to watch your step with him. Anyway, even if the package is a bit damaged, we'll have delivered the goods."

Some few kilometers farther along they left the main highway and turned onto a narrow twisting road that led up into the hills. Another two kilometers, then left, where unmarked wooden posts brought them onto a tree-lined graveled drive. A long low stucco house hugged the side of the hill behind a walled enclosure. The driver got out and pulled at the bell hanging beside the gate. It clanged, the sound echoing as there were footsteps, and the gate opened to admit the station wagon. The gatekeeper, a swarthy Indian, followed the car as it drew up in front of the house, then unlocked the door and stood waiting as the two men handed the Doctor out. The Indian stepped forward.

"You know what to do with him? The big man will be along later."

He nodded, took the Doctor by the arm, and started to lead him into the house. The two men outside dusted off their hands.

"That's a job done." They got back into the car. The driver stuck his head out and waved. "*Adios*. Careful with him," and they were off.

Down a long hall to a corner room, the shutters closed against the sun, the Indian made motions toward the bed and held out a dressing gown and pajamas. The Doctor shook his head but the Indian paid no attention. Too utterly weak, too tired to resist, the Doctor allowed himself to be undressed and helped into bed. He could no longer think, only grateful for present comfort, blessed relief as he shut his eyes and lay back against the pillows.

Sometime later he woke as the Indian came through the door carrying a laden tray. Food. He'd been too exhausted to remember how hungry he'd been lying in the cellar, even now food seemed unimportant, but the Indian set the tray on a table beside him and lifted him up. There was wine in a carafe and a bowl of steaming stew. Almost unconsciously the Doctor began to eat and drink. The Indian watched until the bowl was empty. Still saying nothing, he nodded as if in approval, removed the tray, and drew curtains across the shutters as the Doctor fell asleep again.

Toward the end of the afternoon Dr. Hartung woke in a room still darkened behind the heavy curtains. His mind, however, was clearer, his body still bruised and shaken, but now, thanks to food and rest, he began to remember the events of yesterday. Starting out to join his wife in Taxco, he'd stopped at the dig and gone up to investigate the hillside cave. Little by little things fell into place, his discovery of the boxes and of the cleft in the rock. The cleft, that was the important thing, for surely there must be treasure in the second cave, the treasure he'd been looking for, hoping for. For some minutes he felt almost triumphant, but then his mind clouded again. Those men, his struggle to escape, the terrible hours spent alone in the cold cellar room. Nothing made any sense. And now, where was he? How had he come to this place? Tortured, trying to reason it all out, he turned in his bed as the door opened and a very large, very fat man came through and walked over to stand beside him, calling for the curtains to be pulled and the shutters opened. The man waited until this was done and the two men were alone in the room.

"I trust, señor, we've made you comfortable here. I must introduce myself, Luis Gómez, at your service."

The man spoke English with a heavy accent. Dumbly the Doctor looked up at him.

"We've not met before, though I know of your distinguished reputation. It is a privilege to have you in my house, although I regret the circumstances that brought you here."

Still too bewildered to speak, the Doctor watched as the big man lowered himself into a chair.

"Perhaps I should explain. I own a small interest in the Vista del Rey Hotel. Two of my men were there this morning. Walking through the old sugar cellars they found a man lying hurt in one of the storerooms. Not knowing what to do, they brought you here. On receiving their report I drove out from town this afternoon. Meanwhile I ordered my servant to take care of you. He is a good man, but dumb, as you may have discovered. On my arrival he showed me papers carried in your pocket and I realized how eminent a guest I was entertaining."

"I . . . I am very grateful . . ."

"Please, you must not tire yourself. I only wanted to assure you that you were safe and in good hands. Perhaps later in the evening or even tomorrow morning we can talk."

"But my wife. She expected me to join her in Taxco. She will be worried. I must get word to her."

The big man spread his arms wide.

"I regret, señor, we have no telephone here in my mountain retreat, but, if you give me the Señora's address I will send someone to the village. Better, perhaps, not to alarm her, simply say you are delayed."

Too weak to do more than murmur the names of their Taxco friends, the Doctor sank back as the fat man rose and the door closed behind him.

Packing his bag on Wednesday morning, Henry Cooper threw in a pair of colored slacks, a doubtful present from his sister, but appropriate in Acapulco sport circles, bathing trunks, a white dinner jacket, shirts, underwear, adding binoculars and a small pocket-size tape recorder. Bag closed and a note written to his housekeeper, he went down, loaded his car, and drove out of the city on the road to Cuernavaca. He drove fast but all the while he turned over in his mind the problems ahead. He had no clear idea of just where to start. The answer might well be in Acapulco rather than in Cuernavaca. His own friends, Arabella, the Señora, and the casual acquaintances he'd made, could hardly be supposed to know much of the seamy side of Cuernavaca life, nor did he want to go to the police, who might resent outside interference. Better, perhaps, to get in immediate touch with Verdes, the man whose name had been given to him at the Ministry.

In any case the day was fine and the air cleared as he left the city limits. Sooner or later measures would certainly have to be taken to cut down the pollution or life would be intolerable for any who lived and worked in the capital. Meanwhile the factories belched forth their smoke and behind him a dusty pall lay over the city.

Coming down into Cuernavaca, he parked his car in the main square and went to a corner telephone booth. Taking a piece of paper from his pocket, he dialed the number of his contact, who answered at once, proposing they meet at a small cafe down one of the side streets. Verdes would be sitting at a table outside reading a newspaper.

Walking across the crowded square, Henry found the street and the cafe halfway down the hill. A small man laid down his paper as Henry approached. *"Buenos días, señor."*

*"Buenos días.* I hope I've not kept you waiting."

"Not at all." The two men exchanged compliments and ordered drinks, then proceeded to the business in hand.

"I have two or three names for you, señor, names of men we've been watching for some time, so far with no result." He handed over a scrap of paper, which Henry examined.

"This man Gómez with an address on the Calle Costanza. What about him?"

The other man smiled. "I thought that would catch your eye. Señor García told me you were there at Señora Martínez's on Friday. Gómez lives in the house just opposite, moved in last year. A very large fat man, made a lot of money in real estate, supposed to own shares in the Vista del Rey Hotel and some dance halls in Acapulco. We've nothing on him but he has fingers in a good many queer pies."

"You know there was a murder in the Calle Costanza on Friday? I got there soon after."

"Yes, the police believe they've finally identified the man, a worker from a dig on the Taxco road."

"As I remember, the house across the way looked closed. I stood in the crowd for a few minutes before the dead man was taken off, didn't notice anyone of your fat fellow's description around. Any suggestion Gómez might be involved?"

"Probably not. He would go in for bigger game. But the police aren't satisfied. I nosed about this morning, talked with the Captain in charge of the case. They were trying to reach a Dr. Hartung, who runs the dig, but he's away somewhere. No, there's nothing to connect Gómez with the murder, but you never know."

"I thought I'd steer clear of the police here. Any use my talking to the Captain?"

"Don't think so right now. You know the priest, Father Rodríguez, don't you?"

"I've met him at the Señora's."

"He might tell you more than he told the police. He gave them the tip about the murdered man's identity."

"Surely you can't suspect the Father?"

"Not suspect, but it was queer the man fell on his doorstep. The Padre has a reputation for helping down-and-outers, though he's always been on the right side of the law. Why don't you pay him a call?"

"Glad to, if you think it would help."

"About Acapulco. Gómez has connections there, we know that. If you are lucky enough to mix with the Mendes crowd, you might pick up some clues."

"I've a pretty good introduction there."

"Splendid. You know where to get in touch with me. I'll be around. Now what about lunch? Food's not bad here."

The two men had another round of drinks, followed by an excellent meal. Verdes was good company. Henry enjoyed his stories of undercover work among smugglers, subversives, and drug peddlers. They sat talking over coffee until it was time for Verdes to take the afternoon plane to Acapulco.

"If you get anything on Gómez, don't worry about the other names I gave you. Time enough to haul them in if we make a good catch."

They parted and Henry walked back up the hill to his car. He was tempted to call Arabella, but thought better of it lest she make some excuse not to dine with him. He knew he must go very slowly there, but he realized that his own feelings were pretty well involved. This was a girl with gaiety and courage, a girl to share life in the service and enjoy it. Whatever had happened in the past made no difference. He'd had a few adventures himself.

A couple of hours to kill before paying his call on the priest, so he drove out to the pyramid on the edge of town. The Teopanzalco pyramid could not compare in size or situation with those near Mexico City. It stood, as if shame-faced, in a huddle of shanties, small shops, and gasoline stations, but it still had a kind of ruined grandeur. Henry paid the small entrance fee and walked across to the base, then climbed the crumbling steps. Hard to picture what it must have looked like alone here with the hills as background. He imagined a procession coming out from the small village of Cuernavaca, headed by the priests who mounted the stairs, the people standing below looking up as the sun struck the altar and the bloody sacrifice began.

Curious to think that over in Europe cathedrals were being built to the glory of God while here human beings were killed to appease the terrible deities who ruled the sun and stars. True enough, dark deeds were done everywhere in the name of religion. Not too much difference between Christian and heathen. Even today slaughter and killing still went on and wicked men found means to gain power and wealth, preying an innocent and ignorant people, perverting them for their own ends.

In any event he, Henry, supposed he'd best do his small share in righting the wrong at hand. He did not feel very heroic. It was an ugly business without trumpets or banners, but there it was, a job to be done and, like the old knights, the hope of a beautiful maiden rewarding him at the end.

It was four o'clock when Henry drove down the Calle Costanza and stopped in front of Father Rodríguez's house. Before ringing the bell he stood for a minute on the steps to look across the street. The shutters of the house opposite were closed, but smoke rose from what he supposed must be kitchen and servants' quarters. A side gate opened and a garden boy, bigger than Pepe, came out trundling a bicycle, looked curiously at Henry's car then rode off down the hill.

"*El Padre? Sí, señor.*" The Indian woman who came to

the door ushered Henry down a narrow hall to the priest's study. Father Rodríguez rose to greet his visitor.

"I apologize, Father, for coming unannounced."

"Not at all, Mr. Cooper. It is good to see you in Cuernavaca again. Won't you sit down? Can I offer you tea, a cold drink?"

"Tea, if it's not too much trouble."

"Indeed, no. I take it myself at this time, habit I learned in my student years in England."

Picking up a bell on the desk, he rang. "Tea, María, for the Señor and myself, milk too." He smiled. "In spite of other years spent in the Orient I prefer my tea as the English drink theirs."

The two men chatted for some minutes, Henry speaking of his pleasure at seeing the Señora at the embassy on Monday evening, hoping she had not been too tired after her trip to the city.

"On the contrary. I am sure she enjoyed herself. She goes out too seldom."

Henry put down his cup. "You know this town so well, Father, I've come to ask your help and advice."

The priest's eyes, clear and light, looked into Henry's.

"The matter is serious?"

"It may be, Father. Can you tell me anything about a certain Luis Gómez, who lives here on your street?"

"A big man who comes and goes in large motorcars, keeps much to himself. I know him by sight, that is all. He has no contact with his neighbors and would hardly be interested in a forgotten old priest."

"I should tell you, Father, his name has been given me at the Ministry of Justice. There are rumors there of his being connected with various illegal activities, some of which concern the interests of my own government."

"You are investigating these activities, Mr. Cooper?"

"Only trying to gather information. The situation is complicated. We do not know who or how many individuals or groups of individuals are involved. It would be useful if key figures could be identified."

"These activities. Drugs, I suppose."

"Drugs and illegal exports, guns, even national art treasures."

"And you think this man Gómez may be part of some criminal ring?"

"We suspect him, but lack real evidence."

"I had hoped that here in Cuernavaca we might be spared the evils you speak of. It was perhaps too much to think we could escape. I should have known there is no escape from the forces of darkness, no escape except to fight them with the forces of good. I am an old man, Mr. Cooper, but I am at your disposal."

"Tell me, Father, have you any explication for Friday's murder?"

The priest looked startled. "The police were here yesterday. I gave them what information I had. By now the identity of the dead man should be known."

"I'm told the police are still not satisfied. So far they've been unable to reach Dr. Hartung, the man's employer."

"You are very well informed, Mr. Cooper."

"I was here that day and am naturally curious. I should tell you they are also curious in Mexico City. They seem to think there may be more to it than ordinary homicide."

Father Rodríguez pushed his cup to one side. "I would like to protect the informant who told me the murdered man's name. He did not do so under the seal of the confessional, had no part in the crime, but I am reluctant to involve him."

"Suppose this person has more information to give?"

"That I can't tell you."

"It could be important."

"Perhaps. But what can a workman's murder have to do with the bigger evils that concern you, Mr. Cooper?"

"Call it a hunch. A man is murdered here in the street. Gómez lives here in the street. It may not mean anything but there it is."

Father Rodríguez was silent for a moment, then rose to his feet.

"Very well, Mr. Cooper. I will talk again with my informant."

Henry also rose. "I appreciate that, Father. I go to Acapulco first thing tomorrow morning. Perhaps I might call you before I leave."

"I am an early riser, Mr. Cooper. Why not stop here on your way out of town?"

"Believe me, Father, I am most grateful and again my apologies for disturbing you, and many thanks for the tea."

Father Rodríguez walked with him to the door and watched as Henry got into his car and drove off.


Unable to locate Dr. Hartung, the Cuernavaca police Captain had sent men to the dig on the Taxco road, hoping to gather information there. They found the dig deserted, no workmen about. The watchman was there at the gate, but they got little satisfaction out of the old man. He'd seen nothing, knew nothing. On Tuesday he'd had a day off, went to the funeral of an old friend. When he came back Wednesday morning no one showed up at work. The Doctor? He'd not seen him for several days.

In the village the men were equally uncommunicative. Yes,

they'd been paid well enough, but they thought the dig a
useless business, nothing found, and they were ready to go
back to their fields or look for work in town. Pedro the
foreman and two other men had already left. What about
trouble at the dig? Sure, Pedro was a tough man. There'd
been a few fights. Why not? He'd boasted, said he had grand
friends who would make him a rich man one day. Now he'd
cleared off, left his wife, taken two of his pals with him,
ridden away in his fine car. No one, not even his wife, would
miss him in the village.

The police returned to Cuernavaca, made their report, and
there the matter rested. Meanwhile no news of Dr. Hartung.
The servant who came in a few hours each day to clean
could only say her master had told her he and the Señora
would be away for several days. She'd no idea of their whereabouts, Taxco perhaps. He and the Señora had friends there,
but she did not know their names or the address.

Nothing for it, then, but to await the Doctor's return.


Leaving his car in the square, Henry looked impatiently
at his watch. At least half an hour before he could pick up
Arabella at the boutique. Buying a paper at one of the kiosks,
he sat down on a bench, first making sure he was out of
range of the birds who swarmed in the trees overhead. The
birds were silent, however, roosting now in the branches as
the sun set. The lights went on. Henry read the paper from
front to back, smoked cigarettes, and finally, a few minutes
before six, rose to his feet. He walked over, past the res-
taurants at the entrance to the arcade and down to the
boutique on the left-hand side. The shop was crowded. In
the middle of a group of tourists Arabella was showing

dresses and rebozos to middle-aged ladies and their sport-shirted husbands.

Mrs. Harvey came forward. "Mr. Cooper, what a pleasure. You have come for Arabella, a busy girl, as you see."

"I can wait, but I warn you I'm not buying shirts today, Mrs. Harvey. I'm saving my money to take a young lady on the town."

Mrs. Harvey beamed approval and offered him a chair next her desk. It seemed an eternity before the tourists were satisfied, the dresses tried on, bundles wrapped, and their bills paid. Mrs. Harvy chatted happily away, Henry paying scant attention. Just as Arabella turned to come toward them, another party of eager customers arrived, a harassed-looking father, the usual anxious mother, and two teen-age girls.

Henry looked at Mrs. Harvey in despair.

"Never mind. I'll see to them. You take Arabella along." The good soul bustled forward, said a few words to Arabella, and soon had the party buried in mountains of embroidered garments, shawls, and clanking jewelry. Ignoring Arabella's faint protests, Henry grabbed her by the arm and led her out the door.

"I don't know that I like such masterful men."

"You'd done enough for the tourist trade. Time you concentrated on a poor government servant."

Henry stopped at the first sidewalk cafe. "Now we're going to sit down right here, have a nice cold drink, and forget about everyone but ourselves."

"You take a great deal for granted, Mr. Cooper. How do you know I've no other plans for this evening?"

"You can't have. If you've snared one of those fat tourists I'll shoot him through his embroidered pocket. Besides it's too fine an evening to waste and I'm off to Acapulco tomorrow. I need inoculation against those movie sirens I'll meet."

Arabella laughed. "Just this once, then. The shop stays open late, you know. I can't make a habit of playing hooky."

"Good. Now we've heaps of time until dinner. When you've finished that drink what about a stroll in the Borda Gardens?"

"I'm sure the gates will be closed."

"Knowing Mexico, I should think they leave them open all night. Let's have a look."

"I've been in the shop all day, Henry. I should go home, change my clothes. Considering the Acapulco sirens, I can't go out with you like this."

"You look fine, but there'll be time after we've seen the gardens. I've a table engaged for eight. My car is here in the square, or would you rather walk? It's not too far."

Arabella took a last sip of her drink. Under Henry's cock-sure manner she sensed something quite different. She knew so little about him, yet she knew also she found him oddly disturbing, so much so she was a little shaken by her own feelings as she rose and walked with him down the street.

The entrance to the Borda Gardens, all that remained of the summer palace of the Emperor Maximilian and his wife Carlotta, lay just opposite the cathedral. The gates stood ajar and the guardian looked after them indulgently as they went through. The moon was not up yet, but here and there lights showed among the old trees. The rocky paths wound in and out among neglected rosebushes and shrubs whose perfume hung heavy in the air. Broken marble steps led down the hill flanked by blind-eyed, moss-covered statues. They went on until they found a bench looking out over the town. It was very quiet in the garden.

"Poor Carlotta. She was so happy with Maximilian. They came here often those first years. In Mexico City they were always watched, spied on. They were so young, so silly, I suppose. But think of coming from Vienna to this strange land. Maximilian tried his best but he was weak—those blond whiskers, a pretty man. He sent her home, you know, before the end. She went mad, lived shut up for years and years."

Arabella gave a little shiver as Henry moved closer to her.

"It's ghost-ridden here, Henry."

Henry said nothing as Arabella felt arms around her, strong arms.

"Sometimes it seems I'm a ghost myself."

"Was it so bad there in New York?"

"My own fault, really. I was young too and silly. No excuse, though. It's only one feels empty afterward." She looked up, smiled uncertainly, "He had blond whiskers too. Funny, isn't it?"

"Good thing I have brown hair, sometimes shave twice a day. Come along. Put on that dress you wore Friday at the Señora's. We're going to lay ghosts tonight. You remember Kipling's old jingle, 'The dead they cannot rise, so you'd better dry your eyes and you'd best take me for your new love.'"

Henry took her arm and together they walked back through the garden and out up the street to the square.

Knowing he must talk again with Pepe, Father Rodríguez walked across to the Señora's before dinner, sat with her in the garden, and listened to her account of the dinner at the embassy and of her meeting with the Minister of Justice. She had been impressed by his sincerity but disturbed at his suggestion that Cuernavaca might be infected with the prevalent crime wave.

"We who live behind walls cannot believe such things go on outside. The murder on Friday shocked me very much. Poor man. Is there any fresh news from the police?"

"They are still investigating. The Captain called on me yesterday afternoon. I think they have an idea the man may have come from our friend Dr. Hartung's dig. There'd been trouble there among the men. Have you heard from the Hartungs since your return?"

"No, I believe he and his wife are away visiting friends. The Doctor is such a good man, but simple like many scientists, so absorbed in his work, quite likely he never noticed any trouble. He's so anxious to find that elusive treasure."

The two old friends talked for some minutes longer until the priest rose to leave.

"I'll say a word to Pepe if I may, ask him to come by after dinner. We've some work to go over together."

"You've done wonders for the boy, Carlos. His English improves every day. I brought some books back from the city for him. I'll tell Conchita to fetch them so you can take them along."

Armed with his parcel, Father Rodríguez stopped by the kitchen door, where Pepe was helping Marta to sort out a basket of salad and vegetables from the garden. Telling the boy he had some new books to show him later in the evening, the Father went through the back gate to his house.

Pepe had had an uncomfortable day. Here was his chance to tell the Father what he had seen the night before, but what would the Father say, would he scold him, tell him it was no business of his? Pepe was afraid of the Fat Man. Beppo said he had a bad temper, flew into terrible rages. What would happen if he knew the boy opposite had climbed up a tree to spy on him and told tales of visitors coming and going at midnight?

Small wonder the boy almost dropped the plates when he carried them in for the Señora's dinner. Conchita was angry with him, but Marta hushed her up, said couldn't she see the boy wasn't well. She'd give him a good dose tomorrow.

Thankful when dinner was over and his work finished, but still very fearful, Pepe went across to knock at the priest's back door. Before he knew it he had poured out the whole story to Father Rodríguez, told how he had wakened in the night, heard noises, and had climbed the tree, how he had seen Pedro and another man go into the Fat Man's house while a third man waited outside in a second car. He could not hear anything that was said. They came out some minutes later and both cars drove away. Father Rodríguez listened quietly, asked a few questions, made some notes, then he got up, handed one of the new books to Pepe, and told him to go home.

The boy looked uncertainly at the Father.

"Go home, Pepe, and sleep well. Don't worry. We will talk of this again tomorrow."

Left alone, Father Rodríguez regretfully decided the matter was too serious and Pepe must tell his own story to the police. There was no justification for concealing important evidence, especially evidence that might connect the man Gómez with Pedro and Friday's murder. The police Captain was a decent man and would not be hard on the boy, who was already very frightened. Let him rest tonight, and he would take him along to the station after talking with the young American, who must also be told of this latest development. Father Rodríguez sighed as he put out the lights and went in to bed. Perhaps the Minister of Justice had been right and Cuernavaca could not escape its share of creeping evil.

In his small hotel room Henry Cooper awoke feeling decidedly cheerful. The evening had been a success and the ghosts had been well and truly laid to rest. He and Arabella had dined in a quiet restaurant on the edge of town and they had talked quietly, Henry telling her about his work, the posts he had held, the advantages, even the minor disadvantages, of service life.

"You're a good salesman," she said.

"I have a good product to sell and I'm trying desperately to interest a prospective client," he had replied.

Arabella in turn had talked of herself, of her parents, divorced and remarried so that independence had come too early in her life. "Even at college I was at loose ends, confused. Later, after I found a job, I picked up with the wrong man. No reason, there were others I might have chosen. My friends disapproved and they were right. The affair ended badly. I blamed myself. He really wasn't worth blaming. It had all been quite shabby and commonplace but I was hurt and angry. I came away, as far away as I could, worked for a bit in Mexico City, then heard of the job with Mrs. Harvey. She's been very good to me. Mine's not an interesting story, I'm afraid. It's all happened so often before. Now things are better. You know I can laugh at myself. I did laugh there in the garden, didn't I?"

"Yes, you laughed and we buried that whiskered gentleman with your laugh. You see, you're laughing again."

The rest of the evening had been comfortably gay. The moon, a lover's moon, shone down on them as they drove

back into town, and, as he left, Arabella raised her face for
Henry's kiss.


Anxious to get on with the day's business, Henry hoped he
could dig out enough in Acapulco to justify stopping in
Cuernavaca again on his way back to the city. A conscientious
officer, he realized that personal affairs must be put aside for
the moment, but he sang to himself as he shaved, dressed,
had a quick breakfast, and drove off to keep his appointment
with Father Rodríguez.

While Henry was talking with the priest, another interview
was about to take place in the house among the hills. Dr.
Hartung woke late, considerably refreshed by a long night's
sleep. The silent servant brought his breakfast and left. After
a second cup of strong coffee the Doctor felt comparatively
clearheaded though still confused by the events of yesterday.
Gradually some things came into focus. All very well to lie
here in this comfortable room, but he must see his rescuer,
Señor Gómez, thank him, and go home as soon as possible.
He'd no idea what had happened to his car, perhaps the
Señor could arrange transport of some sort. He must get in
touch with his wife, tell his story to the police, go back to the
dig, and, most important of all, open up the second cave. At
the thought of treasure that might be waiting there his hands
trembled. Foolish to expect too much, but how wonderful if
his hopes were realized, the treasure found, the treasure he'd
sought for so many months. His mind whirling, he scarcely
noticed Señor Gómez had come into the room until the big
man spoke.

"*Buenos días, Doctor*. I trust you slept well."

"Yes, yes." Still very much excited, "You've been very

kind. I cannot impose on you any longer. I must go home at once. My wife—so many things to see to."

"We were able to reach Señora Hartung. She seemed quite reassured, said there was no reason for your coming to fetch her in Taxco. She would be returning with friends tomorrow. I did not wish to alarm the Señora. I said there'd been difficulties at the dig. We'd met by chance and you'd decided to stay here with me near the site."

Not entirely satisfied, the Doctor looked up at Gómez, then smiled. "I'm afraid my wife knows I'm apt to put everything aside where my work is concerned. But I must still go home today, talk with the police, then get back immediately to the site."

"You've had a bad shock. You should rest a little longer, Doctor."

"Thanks to you, I'm quite rested. No, I must leave. There are reasons, important reasons."

"You spoke of the police. What exactly will you tell them?"

"Oh, the police. Of course that's important, but it's the site I'm worried about. So much may have happened there."

"Would it help to tell me about your worries. I have influence in many quarters. Perhaps I might be of assistance."

The Doctor hesitated. He knew little about this man Gómez, but he'd been so kind, rescued him from that horrible place, taken him here to his own house. Suddenly the floodgates opened and he poured forth the story of the caves, of the workman's finding the hidden entrance, of his going himself to the dig Tuesday morning, his discovery of the mysterious boxes, and, his eyes glistening, of the second aperture behind which he guessed treasure might be hidden. "Treasure, señor, think of what that means. It will be my own discovery, one I have dreamed of, worked for."

"You examined the boxes in the first cave, Doctor?"

"Not really. There was a kind of white powder on the floor. I put a little in my handkerchief to show the police, supposing there might be drugs concealed there. One reads of such things, dreadful to think about."

"The men who took you away. Did they know what you had found?"

"That part's pretty hazy. I must have said something, threatened them, and that started the fight."

"Did it ever occur to you, Doctor, what the police reaction would be to your information?"

"I don't know, that's their affair. It's the dig I'm interested in."

"That, of course, but it's very likely their first act would be to seal the cave and forbid any further work on the site."

"You mean the digging would have to stop, that I could not go on to open the second cave?"

"Probably not for some time."

"But that's impossible!"

"The police are not archaeologists, Doctor, especially the Cuernavaca police. I hardly think they would understand your impatience to look for imagined treasure."

"But the authorities gave me permission to dig where I liked on the property."

"A criminal case would take precedence, I'm afraid."

"This, this is very disturbing."

"Would you allow me a word of advice? The men who attacked you, when they know you escaped from the cellar, and they must know this already, they will be very frightened. Very likely they have run off, left the village. If they belonged to a smugglers' gang or had knowledge of anything hidden in the cave, they won't wait for the police. Then too there's the danger to you, to your wife, once information is given. If my men had not found you yesterday, who knows? Murder comes easily to such people."

"But what must I do?"

"For the moment I would say, nothing. Go off on holiday perhaps. Later the caves will still be there. You need not worry. They'll be empty of boxes when you come back. Too risky otherwise. Oh, your car has been found, by the way. One of my men saw one parked in front of your house last night, thought it might be yours because of the foreign license. It was left unlocked so he checked the registration. I told him not to bring the car up here, I'd see that you got home."

"Seems strange they didn't make off with the car."

"Those rascals who abducted you probably didn't want a stolen car added to other counts against them."

"Señor Gómez, you really believe the police would close the cave?"

"I'm sure of it, even more sure that, by going to them now, you may be putting both yourself and the Señora in grave danger."

"How can I explain all this to my wife? What can I tell her?"

"Tell her the truth, that you are uneasy about affairs at the site, that the men were giving trouble and you thought best to stop work there until things simmered down and a new crew could be assembled."

"My wife is a clever woman. She may be hard to convince."

"But why? It is the truth. Even your bruises can be explained. The men were insolent. One struck you. As for your coming here, that also is easily accounted for. I came to visit the dig, met you as you left, we talked together, and I persuaded you to come home with me. A small lie, perhaps, but again, why alarm the Señora?"

"I must think about this, Señor Gómez. How can I abandon my work just as discovery is at hand?"

"It might only be for a short while. Consider the alternatives, Señor Doctor. The cave sealed, and, please believe me, the dangers involved. These men or the people they work for will stop at nothing, you, your wife, even your friends. Their nets spread wide. Later it will be different. Once they are satisfied no complaints were raised, you can return, hire new help, and go on with your business."

As a young man in Norway, Dr. Hartung had lived through the occupation and had seen the Germans' systematic cruelty to hostages and captives. Playing his own small part in the resistance, he had been lucky not to fall into their hands, but the fear of violence had stayed with him. He knew enough to realize Mexicans had a heritage of violence, violence of a different sort, emotional and unpredictable. The danger Gómez suggested frightened him, and the idea of any damage to the caves or their being sealed was unthinkable. As he listened he turned over the risks in his mind. Finally, and reluctantly, he was forced to admit his host might be right and silence, difficult though it would be, the better part of valor. His wife would object, his friends and the authorities might wonder, but, if the delay were not too long, the prize at the end would be worth waiting for.

"Very well, señor, I will do as you suggest. It seems I have no other choice."

"You have made a wise decision, Señor Doctor. Now I know you are anxious to get back to Cuernavaca. A car will be at the door whenever you are ready. I am leaving myself on a short trip, but I hope we may meet again under happier circumstances. I wish you all success when the caves are finally opened and the treasure found."

The two men shook hands, the Doctor expressing his gratitude while his host demurred. "It was nothing. I am only glad to have been of assistance to so distinguished a guest."

His clothes, neatly brushed and cleaned, were on a chair. The Doctor got up and dressed, refusing the help of the servant. His legs felt a bit wobbly, his mind also, but he told himself there was nothing for it but to heed Señor Gómez's advice, so he went out, got into the waiting car, resigned to the inevitable.

The road from Cuernavaca to Acapulco runs almost straight for two hundred and fifty miles through farming country without stops except for the toll booths. It is not a very interesting road, nor was there much traffic so early in the morning. Henry drove almost mechanically, turning over what Father Rodríguez had told him. Here, perhaps, was a definite link between Gómez and the murder of the dig worker, else why would the dig's foreman, Pedro, have paid him that midnight visit? As reported by Pepe, Pedro had been mixed up in trouble at the dig, a bad lot by all accounts. What could the man Pablo have discovered at the dig—gold, perhaps? The coin found in his pocket might be an indication, but would that be reason to have him killed? Gómez's name was on the watch list, right enough. Henry wondered what the police would make of Pepe's story. The boy would be vouched for by the priest, but would they believe such flimsy evidence? In any event this was more or less a local affair unless Gómez could be tied in with the drug racket. The Minister had told Henry such men had fingers in illegal exports of all kinds, and the fellow was certainly suspect. Poor Dr. Hartung, eagerly digging out his bits of pottery. Suppose gold was actually found, what a tragedy for him if it should be stolen, snatched away. Curious to see what the po-

lice would come up with. There was another good reason
for stopping at Cuernavaca on the way home. And then, as
the miles flew by, Henry thought again of Arabella, of the
life they could make together, the wonder of finding such a
girl. There'd been others before, one or two rather torrid
affairs happily ended, with no hard feelings either side, but
this was quite different, had been so from the first. There was
a shared certainty, a happy-ever-after assurance about it. Love
at first sight, a romantic concept, one he'd never really believed in, but now his spirits soared and he sang to himself.

The hours sped along with the miles. The broad farmlands
ended where the town of Las Cruces huddled at the base of a
steep hill. Reminding himself that breakfast had been early
that morning, Henry stopped at a roadside cafe, ordered coffee and a sandwich, topped off with a glass of beer. Taking
out his notebook, he checked names and addresses, finished his
quick meal, and got back into his car, driving up the hill from
the crest of which the great blue bay of Acapulco spread
out before him. Drawing off to one side, Henry looked down.
There, in the shelter of the curve, Cortes had built ships to
scour the coast and later Drake and Morgan had hidden, waiting to sail out and attack the Spanish treasure galleons bound
home from Manila. Now white pleasure yachts and flocks of
small craft, like gulls, dotted the shore.

As he came down into the town, he passed a wide beach.
It was the hour of siesta. Many of the bathers had gone
home, but some brown bodies were stretched out on the sand
and others were picnicking under gaily colored umbrellas.
Opposite, the street shone in the sunshine that glistened on the
glass of bright shopwindows. Farther along ran a line of
hotels, each more elaborate than the next, great wedding cakes
trimmed with flowered balconies and striped awnings,
gleaming motorcars parked in their front driveways. In a

few hours the town would awake and crowds would surge to swim, to buy, to gather on the piers where smart launches would take them out to boats in the harbor.

Henry thought of Drake, wondered what that splendid old sea dog would think of this pleasure-driven resort, a far cry from the deserted beaches where his men came ashore to fill their water casks and sort their booty.

Choosing one of the recommended smaller hotels, Henry went in, gave his name to a slick-haired clerk, and was ushered up to a room looking over a side garden. No use calling the Mendes house until later, but he rang his contact, Verdes, to report his arrival.

"Any fresh news?"

"The Dr. Hartung came back to Cuernavaca this morning, told the police he'd met Señor Gómez at the dig, spent the night with him at his villa in the hills."

"You don't say!"

"He explained there'd been trouble with the men and he was closing down the dig until he found a new lot."

"A queer story—true, you think?"

"The police seemed satisfied. They asked the Doctor to identify the murdered man, but he couldn't help much, said he might be any one of his men. They looked much alike."

"That's probably so. I'm sure the Doctor's honest enough, but he's a scientist, a bit naïve. Have the police checked on Gómez?"

"He's off somewhere on his own, left the house before the Doctor."

"Gives you something to think about, doesn't it? I'm hoping to get in touch with our friend Mendes, so I may be busy this evening. Unless I run into trouble I'll ring you first thing tomorrow."

"I'll be here, señor, same number. You can reach me any time."

Henry unpacked his suitcase, hung up his clothes, and lay down on the bed. It had been a long drive and he slept for an hour or more, then woke and asked the hotel operator to put in a call to the house of Señor Mendes. A servant answered.

"*Residencia Mendes.*"

"*Señor Mendes, por favor.*"

A crisp voice came on the line. "*Secretaria de Señor Mendes.*"

Naming himself, Henry explained that his friend Monsieur Bertrand of the French Embassy suggested he call.

"May I have your number, señor? I will inform Señor Mendes. He will ring you back."

Minutes later. "Ah, Mr. Cooper. I'm delighted you called. How is my friend Jean?"

"Very well indeed. He sent you his thanks for a splendid evening."

The other laughed. "We've enjoyed many together. You are staying long in Acapulco?"

"Only a few days."

"Then we must arrange something at once. You are busy tonight?"

"It's very kind of you, Señor Mendes. I only wanted to give you Jean's message."

"No, no, any friend of Jean's is welcome at my house, and it falls well. I am giving a little party this evening, supper, some dancing and swimming at the pool. I can promise you the girls will be pretty."

"You tempt me, señor."

"Good. Nine o'clock. Dress as you like. You have a car?"

"Yes."

"Your doorman will tell you where to find my place."

"*Muchas gracias, señor.*"

"You speak Spanish, even better than my poor English. Till then—*esta noche.*"

Knowing that he was in for a late night, Henry decided that a visit to Acapulco's famed "afternoon beach" and a swim were in order. Pulling out a pair of trunks, he got into his car and drove to that favorite bathing spot already crowded with a good share of the town's population. He undressed in a cabana and walked up the beach to a relatively quiet section, sat for a while watching anxious mothers hauling their children in and out of the water, helped a small boy to build a sand fort, and eyed the improbable cavortings of brown-skinned young men and girls in abbreviated bikinis. There seemed more play going on than swimming. Henry wished for Arabella, called up a delicious picture of an island beach they would have all to themselves, nothing to do all day or all night but be close together, a delicious picture so raising to the blood he got up and ran down, diving into the water. The swimming was good. It seemed he had most of the bay to himself except for the boats and two or three black heads bobbing about nearer shore. He swam for some time before going back to the cabana, reclaiming his car and motoring out toward the residential section. Best to reconnoiter, find Mendes' house before approaching it in the dark. Every kind of modern architecture swarmed behind walls along the sea front, interspersed with a few older villas. More hotels and houses up the hills; probably each had its own swimming pool where the fashionable dipped and lounged rather than consort with ordinary folk on the beaches. Checking the address, he found the entrance to the Casa Mercedes half concealed behind a grove of trees and bright overhanging shrubs.

Turning around, he drove slowly back to his hotel, stopped in the bar for a drink, then went up and rang Verdes again.

"All set with Mendes. I'm dining at his place this evening."

"Watch yourself, señor. He's a slick hombre."

"Right enough. I'll keep my eyes and ears open."

"Dress as you like," Mendes had said. Henry smiled as he took down the pair of canary-yellow slacks from a hanger, laid out his white coat and shirt, and added a wide figured tie. That should do, he decided, for a playboy disguise. When he had shaved and dressed, Arabella would have thought he looked very handsome, all six feet of him. She might even have approved of the yellow slacks. On the off chance he tucked the tape recorder into a side pocket. Too bad, he thought, they don't issue them in shoulder holsters, but the bulge was no bigger than that of a cigarette package and, as a weapon, it might prove useful.

Somewhat reluctantly, knowing that Señora Martínez had the boy's welfare at heart, Father Rodríguez decided to consult with her before taking Pepe to the police. He found her at her desk in the writing room. She listened attentively as he told her of the murdered man's connection with the dig, of trouble there, and the suspicion attached to the foreman Pedro, of Pepe's waking in the night, climbing the tree and seeing Pedro and another calling late at Gómez the fat man's house, and of their subsequent disappearance from the village on the Taxco road as reported by the police.

"What does Dr. Hartung say to all this?" she asked.

"The Doctor and his wife are still away."

"Of course, I remember they must still be in Taxco. But tell me, Carlos, about Pepe. You believe the boy's story?"

"I have always found him truthful."

"That is so, but these men from his own village . . ."

"No connection, I'm sure. Pepe was naturally very frightened, and it was brave of him to come to me, first to say he thought he recognized the dead man as one of the dig workers and then telling me of Pedro's coming here in the night. You know he has a friend Beppo working at the house opposite?"

"Yes, I've met the boy. I believe he and Pepe were at school together."

"I will ask, but I am quite certain that I am the only one Pepe has told about all this. Beppo is older, not too bright. Pepe would be afraid to tell him much."

"And now?"

"I tried to keep Pepe's name out of the business, but I suspect our neighbor Gómez is a doubtful character and this new link with the man Pedro confirms it. I feel Pepe's evidence is important, so, with your permission, I would like to take him to the police this morning."

"You must do as you think best, Carlos. But how dreadful, our street has always been so quiet, so peaceful."

"Unfortunately crime is no respecter of persons or places."

"Yes, that is what the Minister of Justice said the other night. Poor little Pepe. I hope the police will be gentle with him. You've already seen him this morning?"

"Not yet. I'll go now. Who knows, he may enjoy it, feel himself something of a hero."

"We must make sure the servants, Conchita and Marta, hear nothing of this or the whole street will be in an uproar, but do stop on your way home, for I'll be very anxious to know all that happens."

Leaving the Señora, Father Rodríguez went out across the garden to find Pepe. He was very alarmed at going to the police, but the Father persuaded him that he would be doing the right thing and might even help to solve Friday's murder.

"You must not be afraid. I am coming with you, Pepe. The police Captain is a kind man. There will be no trouble if you tell him the truth about everything you saw and heard."

Now, quite excited at the prospect, Pepe changed into his Sunday clothes, and, minutes later, he and the priest set off in the Father's shabby little car. Arrived at the station, they were ushered into the Captain's office. Father Rodríguez explained the reason for their visit and sat back as Pepe, under the Captain's patient questioning, told of recognizing the man Pablo, of hearing noises in the street that woke him, of going out, climbing the tree and seeing Pedro and another man go into Señor Gómez's house, of their coming out and driving away in a truck, followed by still another man who had waited outside in a car.

"You are sure it was Pedro you saw?"

"Quite sure, Señor Capitán. He lives in my village and works for the Dr. Hartung."

"What do you know about him?"

"A big strong man. The people in the village do not like him. He talks loud and drives a large car."

"Have you ever seen him in Cuernavaca before?"

"No, señor."

"Does Señor Gómez have many visitors?"

"My friend Beppo works there in the garden. He told me some strangers came there last week. They drank a lot. Beppo had to go out for liquor. One of the men was so drunk he stayed all night."

"Did Beppo hear what they talked about?"

"No, señor."

"Have you told Beppo what you saw the other night?"

"No, Señor Capitán. I told the Padre, no one else."

"You did not tell Beppo you recognized Pablo?"

"Oh no, señor. I was not sure at first, but later I knew he was the man I'd seen with others in the village. He was drinking with them at the cafe."

The Captain rose. "We've taken notes of what you said, Pepe, and we thank you for coming to us."

Shaking hands with Father Rodríguez, he laid his arm across Pepe's shoulders. "Who knows, *mi amigo,* you may be a detective one day."


Festively attired, Henry set off for the Mendes house. He had a little trouble parking his car, edging it between two gleaming sports models far down the drive. Ahead of him the house was ablaze with lights. He walked up through the open door into a wide hall and out into the garden lit with torches flaring high in the trees. The terrace was already crowded. His host, in a vivid scarlet coat, greeted him cordially. Turning to a spectacular blonde, "This is Mr. Cooper from the American Embassy. Take him in charge, *querida,* see that he has a good time." The blonde, rather overage for her glittery getup, was most solicitous, guided him out to the swimming pool, where a bar was set up and attendants stepped into the water, glasses in hand, to give them to bathers often lying two by two on floating mattresses.

Motioning to a sultry-eyed young woman in a bright sarong, the blonde moved away.

"*Americano, no?*"

"*Sí, señorita.*"

"The first time you come here?"

"The very first."

"You are not swimming?"

"I came out of the water two hours ago. Now I am here to look at the moon and the beautiful women."

"Too many lights here, but over there"—her braceleted bare arm indicated a grove of trees at the left—"let me show you a Mexican moon."

Amused, Henry followed, but the glade was already occupied by two enlaced bodies. Shrugging her shoulders, his companion turned back again toward the pool. Henry stopped by the bar and ordered drinks for them both. More and more people began to arrive. A famous movie star made a dramatic entrance in a spangled top over wide white satin slacks, her escort in a tightly fitting black silk suit to match his slicked hair. She was soon surrounded, holding court until another young woman, in a costume that consisted mostly of scarlet fringe, drew some of the attention away. There was the inevitable shriek as a red-haired girl was tossed into the pool and emerged in dripping chiffon. The party was well on its way.

A portly Mexican came up to claim his companion, so Henry moved off into the crowd, picked up a pretty blonde, lost her, found a brunette. There seemed plenty to go around.

At a given moment there was a drift toward the house, where a lavish buffet was spread in the dining room. Mendes himself came forward, insisting that Henry sit at his table. Mendes had the reigning movie star on his right, and Henry found himself between a curvaceous young woman and a handsome Junoesque lady in black strung with diamonds in judicious places. The food was delicious, indescribable heaps of fat pink shrimp, a huge fish laid out on a silver platter, salads, cold meat in quivering jelly, mounds of sweets and bowls of bright-colored fruits. Waiters poured champagne into gold-chased goblets, and strolling red-sashed guitarists circulated among the tables.

His curvaceous partner offered little interest except for her curves, so Henry turned to the other side. The lady spoke excellent English.

"You come here often, Mr. Cooper?"

"My first visit to Acapulco, señora. This is a very pleasant introduction."

"Yes, my nephew loves to entertain."

"It was very kind of him to have invited me."

"This sort of thing amuses you, Mr. Cooper?"

"It is a welcome change from diplomatic dinner parties, señora."

"That I can imagine. I wish, however, you might have known the old Acapulco, no swimming pools, only the bay, no night clubs, no movie stars, few tourists, big houses, yes, family houses filled with friends and children, a very happy and innocent holiday resort. I grew up here; now I come rarely."

At another table a young man, to wild applause, poured champagne down his neighbor's back.

"You see why, Mr. Cooper."

Turning away, Señora Ramos addressed herself to the heaped food on her plate. Between mouthfuls, "I admit my nephew has an excellent chef."

Conversation languished. Henry, left to himself, looked around. In the far corner an enormously fat man sat next to the siren in the red-fringed dress.

Leaning toward the curvy blonde, Henry asked, "Who is the stout gentleman over there?"

The partner on her other side interrupted her series of giggles. "Señor Gómez, one of our foremost art collectors."

"And a collector of beautiful women, perhaps," Henry remarked.

More giggles on the left.

"And the others at his table?"

"The girls are part of Mendes' troupe, the men, business types, politicos perhaps."

If they were business types, thought Henry, their business must be conducted with brass knuckles and their politics strictly back-room affairs.

Now the tables were breaking up. Out on the terrace a small orchestra had replaced the guitarists and couples were dancing. Señora Ramos refused Henry's invitation, so he gave his curvaceous dinner partner several turns until he surrendered her still giggling to a swarthy beetle-browed fellow in a striped sport shirt. The fun grew fast and furious and the floor was crowded. Henry drifted off, hoping he might have a few words with his host, get some ideas to take away, but Señor Mendes seemed to have disappeared along with the fat man Gómez and his dubious companions.

Strolling down a path through the trees, Henry saw ahead of him a kind of summer house from which came the murmer of men's voices. Curious, he walked toward it, avoiding a light overhead to stand in deep shadow from where he could see Mendes, Gómez, and some others sitting around a table. An attendant came down the path carrying a tray of drinks. Henry drew farther back into the trees, waiting until the man returned to the house. Drawing as near to the summer house as he dared, Henry reached into his pocket and switched on the tape recorder.

Gone now was every trace of Mendes' playboy aspect. This was a different man, sharp-eyed, his thin face flushed with anger. Opposite him sat the great hulk of Gómez rolling a cigar to and fro in his mouth.

"You made a mess of it, you and your stupid bunch of country *porcos*. So you told them to empty the cave and take the boxes of drugs away. They're probably selling them now to the first small-time dealer they find. And then, Gómez, you stage a rescue of that fool of a doctor and bring him into your own house, spin him a tale no child would believe."

A rumble came from the big man. "I tell you, José, the fellow went home thanking me with tears in his eyes."

"And how long before he spills all this to his wife and that whey-faced priest Rodríguez? *Estúpidos*, all of you. Bad enough those idiots kidnaping Hartung, but why the devil did you interfere? You say he's an old man. He wouldn't have lasted long, shut up in that cellar."

"Wait a minute." Gómez took the cigar out of his mouth. "You don't know this doctor. I talked with him. He couldn't care less about the boxes. All he thinks of is finding treasure. He's crazy on the subject, frightened silly when I told him if he went to the police they would close up the cave. He won't say anything. I saw to that."

"Tell that to the fairies," one of the other men broke in. "José is right. It's a bloody mess and no mistake. And if you think you're going to drag any of us into your dirty business, think again."

Mendes motioned the man to be silent. Sitting back now, he spoke slowly and coldly.

"The man Hartung must be taken care of. He knows too much. That will be your job, Pasco. I'll put a trail on Pedro and his pals. As for you, Gómez, you're through. I recommend the first plane out, plenty of nasty work for you farther south. Rico here will see you safely aboard, and wherever you are, if you so much as squeal we'll find you. Take him away, Rico, he smells worse than his cigar."

Gómez's face was gray and his big body shook as he rose to his feet. The man Rico came behind him, reached into both pockets, pulled out a revolver, and threw it on the table, then took the fat man's arm and led him toward the door.

Switching off the tape recorder, Henry shoved it away and edged quickly through the trees, his one thought to get clear of any of the men coming out of the summer house. Emerging finally on the lawn below the swimming pool, he skirted the terrace and rounded the far end of the house. No one took any notice until he came out on the front drive. Here an attendant came up to offer to find his car and bring it to the door.

"*Muchas gracias*." Henry shook his head and walked on down the drive. Thankful to discover he had room to turn the car, he got in and headed toward town. His mind was awhirl with all that he had seen and heard. He must get hold of Verdes, the contact man, at once so protection could be arranged for Dr. Hartung. The tape must be delivered to Mexico City, put into proper hands. He had no illusions now about Mendes and his crew. They were ruthless criminals, capable of murder and almost anything else on the calendar. He admitted to himself he would never have guessed Mendes to be chief of the gang. Gómez looked more the part. Not so tonight, Gómez quaking like a sick elephant as Mendes told him off, and Mendes, playboy mask dropped, appeared the vicious snake that he was. Henry wished he might have faced him later, but that wasn't his business. His own countrymen must take care of him.

Better, perhaps, not to phone Verdes from the hotel. Lights shone from an all-night cafe. Stopping the car, Henry got out, went in past a crowded bar into a back room where a noisy pool game was going on.

"*Teléfono? Sí, señor*, over there in the corner."

Intent on their game, the players paid no attention as he put coins in the slot and dialed.

"I'm on my way back into town. Where can we meet?"

"The sidewalk in front of your hotel. Pick me up there."

Henry made his way out, got back into his car, and drove down the avenue. As he drew up to the hotel entrance Verdes walked toward him. Opening the car door, Henry remarked, "Quick work. As we say, you're Johnny on the spot."

Stopping the car farther along the street, he filled Verdes in on the evening's adventures. The tape recorder burned a hole in his pocket, and he explained he must get it back to Mexico City, the sooner the better.

The other man listened, then, "I'll do the necessary for the Doctor, also make sure the airports are alerted and the harbor police here warned. They may try to get Gómez out by ship. If I might suggest, señor, you could take a plane tomorrow morning to the city. There's a fast one at eight-thirty. You won't find Gómez on board. Mendes will have commandeered a charter flight to get him away. If you permit I'll drive your car back, start when I've lined everything up here in Acapulco."

"Good idea. I'm worried about Hartung, though, he's such a trusting hombre."

"I'll see that men are put onto him at once."

Back again at the hotel, Henry turned the car over to Verdes and went up to his room. Matters were now out of his hands for the moment. A good man, Verdes. As he said, he'd do the necessary all right, though Henry had twinges of regret at missing the planned stop at Cuernavaca. No help for it.

Once the tape was delivered into safe hands his immediate job was finished and time left for more private pursuits.

Dr. Hartung, still very tired and somewhat shaky, arrived at his house about noon. The old cleaning woman prepared him a lunch of sorts, and afterward he lay down on a sofa in the living room. He was awakened by a ring at the door and the old woman shuffling down the hall to answer it. He heard the voice of his wife. Struggling to his feet, he went out to meet her.

"Nils, you look ill. What has happened?"

"No, no, Helga. I am all right, but it's a long story. I've been very worried about the dig, very worried . . ."

"And who is this man Gómez who telephoned me? How did you come to spend the night with him? I never heard of him before."

"He found me at the dig. There was trouble with the men. They knocked me about. Señor Gómez was very kind. He took me to his house, a beautiful house in the hills."

"It all sounds very queer. You look as if you have a fever."

Bustling away, the good lady went out, to come back with a thermometer which she stuck in his mouth.

"I thought so. You've caught a nasty cold. I'll get you to bed at once. You can tell me more later on."

The Doctor followed her obediently upstairs and allowed himself to be undressed and put to bed, his own bed, so comfortable. It was good to be back at home, but he reminded himself of Gómez's warning, of the probability of the police closing the cave and of possible danger for his wife and for him. Yet, how could he keep all this from Helga? It would be hard, very hard. Even in the bad days of the war they had shared each other's worries and fears. This danger Gómez spoke of, as an archaeologist and historian Dr. Hartung knew only too well the Mexican inheritance of violence. The Aztecs had left more behind them than the pyramids. Difficult though it would be, he supposed he must follow Gómez's advice.

Later that evening the Doctor's wife was sufficiently disturbed by her husband's condition to telephone Father Rodríguez.

"Nils is in bed with a feverish cold, I found him here when I got back from Taxco. The cold is not serious, but he talks quite wildly, tells me when he went to the dig the workers attacked him, that a Señor Gómez happened to come by and took him home for the night. I can't make head or tail of it. I wonder, such a good friend, would you stop in tomorrow and have a word with him?"

"But of course I'll come. Have you called a doctor?"

"No, he's resting quite comfortably now. After a night's sleep he should be himself again. It's only, I thought, he would talk more easily with you. He seems to have so much on his mind."

Father Rodríguez himself had a good deal on his mind, some of it concerning the Doctor, so he was only too willing to accede to Mrs. Hartung's request. Accordingly, at ten next morning he parked his small car outside and rang the bell of the Hartungs' house. He did not notice a man sweeping the sidewalk who glanced at him sharply, then went over to speak to a second man across the street. Verdes' message had gotten through the night before and two men were already on duty.

Taken up to the Doctor's room, the priest was shocked at his friend's appearance. Not much sign of the cold his wife had mentioned, but the man looked ill indeed and his greeting seemed forced.

The two chatted for some minutes, then the Father inquired casually for news of the dig, as the Doctor had spoken so optimistically when they met at the Señora's on Friday.

"Yes, but now I don't know. So much trouble, much trouble. I can't go on with it . . ."

"This trouble, can you tell me about it?"

The Doctor looked up at the priest, then down, his fingers moving, plucking nervously at the bed sheet.

"No, no. The dig must be closed, all my work stopped, gone for nothing. I, I had such hopes . . ." His voice broke.

"I think, my friend, you must tell me about the trouble." The Father spoke gently. "Remember I am a priest, your troubles cannot be greater than many others I have listened to."

The Doctor looked up again, his face suddenly clearing.

"That is so, you are a priest. You will not speak of this to others, to my wife. He said, Gómez said there would be danger for her."

"If you will confide in me I will see how I can help you."

The Doctor's words came slowly at first. He was almost incoherent. The Father waited quietly until his friend took hold of himself and the story unfolded, the story of the discovery made in the cave, of the argument with Pedro the foreman, of his abduction and the terrible night spent in the hotel cellar, of his rescue by the two men who took him to Gómez's house in the hills, of Gómez and what he had said, warning him against going to the police lest the caves be sealed and all hope gone of finding the treasure.

"You see now why I must keep silent. Those men, the bad men, might come back. We would not be safe here."

"You feel you are safe now?"

"I'm not sure, not sure at all. Perhaps we should leave, go away, far away." The poor man began to tremble.

"Don't worry, my friend. This trouble, like other trouble, will pass. Trust me. You must rest now. I will come back tomorrow."

Judging quite rightly that the Doctor was in no condition to be told who and what manner of man Gómez might be or any of the complications involved, Father Rodríguez left after cautioning Mrs. Hartung not to question her husband. "We had a good talk, best not to agitate him. I'll be here tomorrow again and we can straighten things out."

The same man was working in the street when the priest went out. He looked after him as the car drove away, and nodded to another keeping watch nearby.

Early Friday morning Pepe opened the Casa gate to pick up the paper. He looked across the street and saw a police car standing outside the Fat Man's house; the front door was open and men were going in and out. Afraid the police would see him, Pepe closed the gate and went back quickly through the garden, took up rake and broom, and set to work, wondering all the while what was happening over the way and if the information he'd given had brought the police there. Had they come to take the Fat Man to prison? There was no sign of him. He must be away. Pepe thought of Beppo, quite sure he'd known nothing of his master's business, but the police might not believe that. There was the cook, too, a cross old woman. Beppo teased her and she'd say anything to get him in trouble. Pepe wished he might speak for Beppo. Unless the police held him, he knew Beppo would come over later and give him the whole story. It wouldn't be long before the news of the police raid would be known up and down the street. Already Pepe heard voices outside and, as he turned to go into the kitchen, his Aunt Josefina came through the back garden gate in a great state of excitement.

"The *policía!* All over the place. They are turning Señor Gómez's house inside out!"

The kitchen was in an uproar now. Conchita, Marta, and Josefina all talking at once.

"One murder leads to another," Conchita said darkly. "Soon none of us will be safe in our beds."

"Who knows the police may have found Gómez, his throat already cut? That cook"—Josefina crossed herself—"I always said she had the evil eye."

"Murder or no," Marta broke in, "the Señora must have her breakfast."

Pepe listened, ate up his bread and drank his coffee, and left, not wishing to be caught up in the conversation. Besides all this would upset the Señora. He must look for the prettiest rose in the garden to put on her tray.

Sometime later there was a ring at the front gate. Pepe opened it fearfully, but it was only last Friday's hero the postman with letters and a package of books to be signed for. The excitement in the street had subsided, the house door opposite was closed now, and the police car had gone. Pepe carried in the mail, gave it to Conchita, and just then the Señora came into the patio. She spoke to Pepe.

"The roses in the far bed may need spraying, and just there"—she indicated with her cane—"I've ordered two new bushes, white, they should do well against the green behind." They walked along together, the Señora making a few more comments and suggestions. She said nothing of this morning's disturbance, nor of Pepe's visit to the police station the day before. Pepe felt, however, that she knew and would not scold or inquire about his waking in the night and climbing the tree to watch what went on across the way. She was a great lady, and a wise one.

The Señora went back into the house, and Pepe worked on through the morning. Just after lunch Beppo appeared. He was full of all that had happened in the house. The police had questioned him and the cook.

"The old *vaca*. They couldn't get anything out of the cow except a lot of chatter. I was scared, but I told them all I knew about the men who came to the house, said I didn't know who they were or what they talked about, so the police finally let me go, told me the house would be closed and I might as well cut off for home."

"But what's happened to your boss?"

"Nothing good, I guess. Anyway I'm not working for him anymore. He was always a disagreeable old bastard. I'm catching the bus up to the village. Jobs are scarce there, so keep your ears open and let me know if anything turns up in town."

Pepe looked after Beppo, glad the police had given him no trouble. He'd miss Beppo, always so cheerful and good-natured, but right now he had other things on his mind.

Father Rodríguez was concerned for his friend Dr. Hartung. The poor man was so credulous. Obviously he had been completely taken in by Gómez, who must have ordered his rescue from the cellar and then frightened him from going to the police by saying the caves would be closed. The Doctor's interest lay in the treasure and it would have been easy to distract his attention from the cache of drugs. A clever man, Gómez, but happily to be brought to justice if the raid on his house was any indication. Now it remained to convince the Doctor that his story must be told to the police. His testimony would be of vital importance and, with the drugs removed, there would be no reason to close the caves or forbid him to continue his work. That elusive treasure—when the second cave was opened he hoped the Doctor would not be disappointed.

Much recovered after a night's rest, quite clear now in his mind, Dr. Hartung was delighted to see Father Rodríguez when he stopped by that morning. They talked at length. At first it was hard for the Doctor to believe Gómez had deceived him, but little by little he realized this must be true. He was still uneasy about the danger that might ensue if he told his story to the police.

"Suppose Pedro or any of the others return?"

"There's little chance of that. If they're not caught they'll have cleared off, moved on to do their dirty business elsewhere. With their chief Gómez out of the picture you may be sure they won't stay here."

The Doctor still hesitated, so Father Rodríguez decided to play his final card. Reaching into his pocket, he brought out a gold coin which he put into the Doctor's hand.

"Spanish gold! Where did you get this?"

"It was found in the pocket of the murdered man Pablo. I asked the police if I might show it to you."

"That man . . . He must have been the worker who discovered the cave entrance. The police asked me about him. I couldn't remember, I wasn't sure, but now . . ." The Doctor's hand closed over the coin. His voice rose. "Think, think what this means! The treasure, the treasure must be there. I knew I was right. This is tremendous. I must get up at once, go to the cave."

"Wait, my friend. Who knows where the man picked it up?"

"No, no, it came from the cave, it must have come from the cave." The Doctor started to get out of bed.

"All in good time. Believe me, if any treasure is there it's now under police protection."

"But that is what I am afraid of. They'll shut the place up, forbid my going in." The Doctor was now almost wild with excitement.

"You're wrong. The police are on your side. Once they hear your story you'll be free to do what you like. It's the criminals they want, criminals who planted drugs there and would have looted any treasure they found. You're not after gold for yourself. Anything you dig up stays here in Mexico. No, if the treasure is there it's as safe as when it was buried four hundred years ago, even safer once you've talked with the police. This I earnestly advise. You will protect your wife, the treasure, and yourself, if you agree."

The Doctor's doubts began to crumble as he looked into the priest's face. "You would not say this unless you believed it. Very well. Tell me what I must do."

"No need for you to go to the station. I'll telephone at once, ask Captain Huelga to come here. He's in charge of the Pablo case, a good man. You can trust him."

"You'll stay with me?"

"If you like. I confess I'm interested myself. I've an idea Pablo intended telling me something of his discovery, the drugs, perhaps, in which he may have been involved. Poor fellow. It's not often I have a penitent murdered on my doorstep."


Henry Cooper went to bed with the precious tape recorder under his pillow, left an early call for breakfast, and caught the eight-thirty plane as planned next morning. The flight was a short one and he arrived at Mexico City airport coming down through the usual blanket of yellow smog. He hesitated whether to report to the embassy before going to the Ministry, but he was too anxious to hand over the tape, so he took a taxi and was in García's office before noon.

"Congratulations, Mr. Cooper. Verdes telephoned us from Acapulco, told us something of your evening's adventures. Gómez got away, but the net is out and our friends to the south will send him home. Don't worry, we'll get him back, though the package may be a little damaged in transport. If he's left to rot down there it's no affair of ours."

"Did Verdes tell you I recorded a tape of Mendes' conversation? I have it here in my pocket."

"Splendid, the Minister is most anxious to see you. We'll take the tape along."

Minutes later they were admitted to the Minister's inner office. Señor Morado shook hands cordially with Henry, who laid the tape on the desk. "A small present, Your Excellency, from Acapulco."

A machine was brought in. Henry described the scene in Mendes' summer house, the men sitting around the table, then the tape came on with the voices of Mendes, Gómez, and the others.

"Let's hear it again. You've taken notes, García? Too bad Gómez got away. Mendes probably sent him off last night, had a plane parked somewhere. Never mind, we'll find him sooner or later."

The three men listened once more, then sat back as García switched off the machine. The Minister turned to Henry. "A fine job, we are most grateful. This gives us enough to go on with. As I told you, if we catch a big fish, others will fall into our net, and Mendes is a very big one."

"I confess, Excellency, I thought Gómez might be the kingpin, but Mendes treated him like a lackey."

The Minister spoke with some bitterness. "Mendes likes to believe he is descended from the conquistadores. He has a nasty way with Indians. It will be my pleasure to show him what one Indian can do. Put a watch on all his associates, García, one of them might lead us to the Cuernavaca murderer." Getting up from his chair, "We must not keep you, Mr. Cooper. I know your Ambassador will want a report. Later I will call on him to express my thanks for your help. You accomplished more than we could have hoped for."

Arrived at the embassy, Henry found the Ambassador had left for lunch, so he had time to put in a call to Arabella, always a lengthy business due to Mexican telephone operators' happy faculty for wire tangling. He finally reached her after some minutes of frantic struggle.

"I'm reporting in. Acapulco sirens notwithstanding, my heart and hand are still yours . . . No, operator, don't cut me off." Cursing, he jangled the phone and heard Arabella laugh as it came on again. "I'll be down on Sunday as early as I can make it. Have to clear things up here, but I've lots to tell you. Save lunch, afternoon, dinner, and all the rest of your life for me."

This time the phone went completely dead. Satisfied his message was delivered, Henry put the receiver down, then went off to catch a bite of lunch and return to make his report to the Ambassador.

The night had been a long one, so it was not until afternoon that José Mendes emerged in swimming trunks and a striped bathrobe to sit beside his pool, now cleaned and emptied of all traces of broken glass and various garments discarded by the evening's revelers. Only one guest, a more or less permanent resident, remained, the curvaceous blonde who had sat beside Henry Cooper at dinner. Mendes, nursing a long restorative drink, said little to her and the blonde fidgeted in her chair, finally getting up to dangle her feet in the water. José was in one of his moods, a nasty one by the look of it. She'd get nothing out of him until tonight; meanwhile she was bored. An afternoon wasted.

The terrace doors opened suddenly to a frightened butler followed by four men, three of them in police uniform, who walked across the lawn to the pool. Startled, the girl gave a scream, got up, threw a robe around her, and ran for the house. Mendes remained sitting as the men came to stand beside him.

"To what do I owe this intrusion, señores?"

The fourth man in plain clothes stepped forward.

"We regret disturbing you, señor, but the police authorities in Mexico City want you there for questioning. The four-o'clock plane is being held. One of us will accompany you as soon as you are ready to leave."

"Questioning? What about? I've no intention of leaving. Tell your police if they have any business with me I'll see them here."

"Sorry, señor. I have my orders."

"You may have orders, but they're mistaken ones. I'll call my friends in the Ministry at once."

"My orders are from the Minister himself. There is just time for you to dress. The plane is waiting."

Mendes got up, shrugged his shoulders. "Very well, we'll make a quick end to this farce. After all, it'll give me a chance for a night on the town."

The plain-clothes man told two of the police to follow Mendes into the house. "Stay with him. Be quick about it and don't let him near a telephone. Bring him down. We'll wait for you in the car."

It was a silent drive to the airport. The plain-clothes man and Mendes boarded the plane, taking seats in the rear. No one took special notice of them, though several passengers were heard grumbling at the delayed departure. As the plane took off Mendes closed his eyes, while his companion sat quietly looking straight ahead.

On arrival they were the last to leave the plane. A police car was waiting on the field and minutes later they drew up at the Ministry of Justice, where they were immediately ushered into García's office.

Here Mendes began to expostulate. This was all absurd. He demanded to see the Minister at once. García made no reply but reached over to the machine on his desk and turned on the tape.

"Listen carefully, señor, and you will see we have ample evidence to hold you on suspicion of drug dealing. Any questions can wait until tomorrow when you will, no doubt, wish to have your lawyer present. You are, of course, at liberty to communicate with him at any time, but I am afraid you must accept the city's hospitality for tonight. We hope that one or two of your associates may be joining you later in the evening."

Paying no attention to his protests, the two police closed around Mendes and led him out through the door.


Dr. Hartung, encouraged by Father Rodríguez, had been very frank with the police. The Captain had listened carefully, notes were taken, and he left telling the Doctor he would return early that evening with a typed statement for him to sign.

"By then we may have later news for you. We've just had a tip as to the whereabouts of your assailants. With luck we'll soon catch up with them."

Dr. Hartung was very glad now that he had talked with the police, especially as the Captain had assured him they intended no interference with his work at the dig. He told his story all over again to his wife after the Captain and the priest left. The poor lady was horrified to think of her husband's dreadful ordeal, but comforted by the thought that the wicked men would be found and punished.


Pedro and his companions were hiding out in the hills. Now and then one of them crept down into the village at night to bring back food and liquor from a terrified wife or girl friend. The men grew restless and quarrelsome.

"You, Pedro, got us into this mess. You're so smart, now get us out of it. Let your fine friend Gómez come across. We've got plenty on him if we sing to the police."

"And who'll believe you? You'd never get away with it. We'd end up in the jug, all of us."

"What about Pablo? There's a good story for them. You'd take the rap for that one. We'd nothing to do with it. Think it over, *amigo*. Use that big brain of yours."

The days wore on. Rations grew short. One of the men caught a lizard, stewed it up. The cave reeked with the smell.

"That's enough. I'm clearing out. Anything's better than this stinking hole." The second man got up.

Pedro lunged forward, reached out, and knocked him flat.

The man lay blubbering in a corner and the other looked away.

It was one of the village women who finally broke down. She was sick, out of money, another baby was due, so, when the police paid one of their daily visits to the village, she told them what she knew, the men were up there, somewhere in the hills. The search was on, and before too many hours the three men were rounded up, taken down, and locked in Cuernavaca jail.

Later the police Captain telephoned Father Rodríguez.

"Tell the boy Pepe we have all three men here, found them hiding in the scrub near the village. Tomorrow we'll ask Dr. Hartung to identify them as his kidnapers. I'm seeing him this evening. One of the men has already talked, pinned Pablo's murder on Pedro, so we may not need Pepe's evidence, but I'll have a job waiting for that junior detective any time he wants it. We couldn't have cracked the case without him."

Delighted to hear of the men's capture, Dr. Hartung brought out glasses and a decanter of brandy, insisting that Captain Huelga join him in a small celebration. They toasted each other, Mrs. Hartung beaming approval. The typed statement was spread out on a table. The Doctor signed, then, over another glass of brandy, "I'm still puzzled about Gómez. What was his motive for deceiving me about the caves, and why did he have me rescued from the cellar?"

The police Captain turned the glass in his hand.

"The explanation, as we see it, is this. Gómez is probably connected with a drug ring. He used the cave in which to hide the stuff preparatory to shipping it away. The man Pablo might have come on the boxes when he discovered the cave entrance. Very frightened, he could have gone down into town to confide in Father Rodríguez. Such a man would be fearful of the police and far more likely to look for help from a priest, especially one known for charity to all and sundry. He was followed and murdered, probably by Pedro or one of his confederates, all of whom were in Gómez's employ. Your visit to the caves and your questions to Pedro threw the latter into a panic, hence the abduction of which Gómez knew nothing until told by Pedro later that night. We know they came to Gómez's house, for they were observed by Señora Martínez's garden boy Pepe. Gómez, a clever man, realized the immediate consequence of so rash a performance as your abduction, so he ordered the rescue and had you brought to his house in the hills. He sensed your real interest lay in finding treasure, so he told you the police would seal the caves for good and all if you went to them with your story. This, he hoped, would convince you to keep silent."

The Doctor shook his head. "You must wonder at my stupidity, but scientists are simple folk, Captain. I'm afraid we are too occupied with our own work, too naïve, too unaware of what goes on around us. We live in a dream world of our own. Lucky for us there are men like you to protect the innocent and credulous. But the man, Gómez, where is he now?"

"I believe he has fled the country. You'll hear no more of him unless one day he can be brought back to justice. There are others, even bigger men, in this business and powerful forces are at work to track them down. We here in Cuernavaca do our small bit, but I can only say your unfortunate experience has helped very much in the larger effort to root out the drug evil. More I cannot tell you."

The Captain rose, shook hands with the Doctor and his wife.

"When you decide to go back to your work at the dig,

let me know. I'll send a couple of strong men along to shovel dirt for you."

On Sunday morning Henry Cooper set out for Cuernavaca in high spirits. In spite of his lawyer's efforts Mendes remained locked up, and various other prominent gentlemen were under house arrest. The Ambassador had been very pleased with Henry's report, which was duly forwarded to Washington.

It was a cheeful young man who appeared at Arabella's door shortly before noon. He swung her into his arms.

"Henry, you go too fast."

"Not fast enough. Here." He reached in his pocket and pulled out a small package. "Try this on for size." He put it in her hand, a ring, an old ring, chased gold set with a single emerald.

"I shopped for it yesterday, thought you'd like it better than the usual Tiffany diamond."

"But Henry . . ."

"No buts." He slid it on her finger. "Fits well, too. The Spanish señorita who wore it must have had as pretty hands as yours."

Arabella looked down at the ring, then up at Henry.

"You really think?"

"I really think."

"It's beautiful, Henry. I . . . I . . ."

"Tears aren't called for." He leaned over, kissed them away. "In case you've any doubts, I love you. I've loved you for ten long days."

"Silly, isn't it? But I love you too, Henry."

"And now we've a lifetime ahead to love each other. That's the best of it. Let's go tell the world about it. Listen, do you hear the bells? They've just heard about us at the cathedral and are ringing a peal."

Mass over, the worshipers were coming out of the church across the way.

"I know, let's call on the Señora. It's really her doing after all, that lunch party on Friday."

The two young people went out hand in hand, jumped into Henry's car, and drove out to the Casa Santa Luiza. Pepe had been given the day off, so it was Conchita who opened the gate, and even that grim dragon smiled at seeing their shining faces. They found the Señora and Father Rodríguez sitting in the patio. Shyly Arabella came forward and sank to her knees beside the Señora's chair. Henry stood silent. Señora Martínez took Arabella's hand in hers and looked at the ring.

"Dear child. So I am to wish you happiness."

Clearing his throat, Henry spoke. "We've come to thank you for bringing us together," then, turning to the priest, "and you, Father, will you give us your blessing?"

"By all means." Father Rodríguez smiled. "I've always heard Americans were what are called 'fast workers,' but I congratulate you both. Happiness is rare. It is good that you have found it."

The Señora insisted that Arabella and Henry stay for lunch. "I take a rest afterward, so you will have the garden to yourselves." Calling for Conchita, she told her to bring champagne.

"Señor Cooper and the Señorita are betrothed, '*estáu comprometidos para casarse.*' Ask Marta to join us. We must drink to their health."

Glasses were brought, the wine poured. Conchita and Marta stood to one side, Marta, overcome, wiping her eyes on a corner of her apron: "*Muy, muy simpático.*" The sun shone down on the flowers, the pool, and crept through the slatted roof of the patio.

The Señora raised her glass. "To Arabella and Henry, a long and joyful life."

The luncheon party was a merry one. After coffee the Señora and Father Rodríguez disappeared, leaving Henry and Arabella together. So much to talk about, so much to explore, but they said little, wrapped in the quiet wonder of their happiness.

Later on Arabella suggested they revisit the Borda Gardens. On a Sunday afternoon there were more people wandering about, but they found a bench hidden to one side where a little fountain trickled from a rusty pipe and bright flowers struggled through the overgrown grass and weeds. Henry told her of his adventures in Acapulco and of his luck in recording the meeting in Mendes' summer house. She laughed at his description of the supper party and held her breath at the picture of him standing in the shadows listening to the men's conversation.

"Suppose they'd caught you, Henry. What would have happened?"

"Something very nasty, I'm afraid, but when the meeting broke up I lit out fast, got in touch with my police contact, left my car with him to drive back, and took the early plane to the city next morning. My job was done when I turned the tape over to the people in the Ministry of Justice."

"And Mendes?"

"They flew him in later that same day and rounded up all the gang except Gómez, who was got out during the night. Mendes was the top man, comes of an old Mexican family, but a very bad hat. There'll be a lot of publicity when he goes on trial, but some of his pals will be sure to talk, and, with

Mendes locked up, the Minister believes a big dent has been made in the drug traffic."

"All thanks to you, Henry."

"I was lucky. I admit I had a few quavers when I stood outside the summer house. They were such a tough-looking bunch. But it was fun really."

"Perhaps. But I'll make sure I'm with you next time you attend a pool party!"

From the Borda Gardens they went to call on Mrs. Harvey, who threw her arms around each and regaled them with rum-flavored tea and sweet cakes. "You won't be leaving me right away, will you?" she asked Arabella.

The girl looked at Henry.

"Now that I've found her I'm not taking any chances. One of those rich tourists might buy her up along with his shirts. I'm sure Mexican weddings can be arranged on twelve hours' notice. You'd make a charming bridesmaid, Mrs. Harvey."

Arabella protested, shook her head. "Pay no attention to him. We're both a little dizzy right now."

"And no wonder," the good lady said. "But I saw the light in his eyes last Saturday when he brought you into the shop. Don't wait too long. Hold tight or time runs away from you."

They promised to tell her as soon as plans were made, and left for an early dinner, as Henry had to drive back to the city. Choosing a restaurant near the palace square, they ordered their meal and the waiter set a jug of sangría on the table.

Over their drinks, "You know Mrs. Harvey had the right idea. Why not be married here? I've some extra leaves on the books. Would your family be horrified if you arrived in New York with a husband?"

"What about your own family? What would they say to your bringing back a wife?"

"Don't worry. They'd almost given me up. They'd welcome you with open arms. Perhaps you feel you should go back to the States, see your friends, family, go through the usual bridal routine. I'm game for anything."

"Neither of us is quite sober, Henry. This has all happened so suddenly. I must cable or telephone my parents about our engagement. That's only fair, afterward—I don't know. I don't like weddings where the divorced wife glares from the pew at her divorced husband. I think, if I can think at all right now, I'd rather be quietly married here, but let's wait a few days, then make a plan."

"I'll have half a dozen for you to choose from when I call you tomorrow, more the next day, but every one will start with wedding bells."

They went off laughing, got into Henry's car, and said a long good night at Arabella's door.


Father Rodríguez had called on Dr. Hartung that afternoon and was delighted to find him completely recovered. He had been to the jail and had identified his abductors. Satisfied they were kept under lock and key, the Doctor was determined to visit the dig next day, fearful lest damage might have been done by Pedro and his men when they went back to empty the cave. He pressed Father Rodríguez to accompany him.

"The police Captain offered to send a couple of men along, but I'm not sure. Better, perhaps that we go alone, take a look around, and see what's to be done, how to go about opening up the second cave."

"You really believe there's treasure hidden there?"

"There must be. That coin was an indication."

"Pablo could have picked it up almost anywhere."

For a moment the Doctor hesitated. The priest sensed he fought against rising doubt. Then he shook his head. "No, no. It had to come from the cave. I do believe in the treasure. I must believe or all my work, all this trouble, goes for nothing. You'll see when we get there. I'll show you the crack in the cave wall. We might dig out enough to peer through. You will come, won't you?"

Somewhat reluctantly Father Rodríguez agreed. He dreaded the Doctor's disappointment if, as he feared, the treasure proved nonexistent. Previous digging in the area had not turned up anything of importance, and he knew that the museum authorities discounted further discoveries. He was anxious for his friend who had staked so much on this project. After his recent ordeal a fresh blow would go hard with him. Still he could not refuse the Doctor's request, and it might be just as well he not go alone if there was nothing to be found but crumbling rocks and dust.

Supplied with a lunch provided by Mrs. Hartung, the two men set off early next morning in the Doctor's car. The Doctor, a rather impulsive driver, swerved around the mountain curves, but they arrived safely on the outskirts of the village near the dig site. Remembering that the boy Pepe had gone up there on Sunday to spend the night with his family, Father Rodríguez suggested he might be of help and glad of a lift back to town. Several inquires finally brought them to Pepe's house, a fair-sized tin-roofed shack set in a garden patch just off the main road. In a side yard a tethered goat held court midst a scattering of chickens, a sow with her pink piglets, and a brown and white dog who kept watch over a baby sleeping in a rope hammock hung between two trees.

Calling to a young girl who came out of the house with a

bundle of wash in her arms, Father Rodríguez got out of the car.

"Pepe? He just left to catch the bus." An older woman spoke over the girl's shoulder, recognized the priest and Dr. Hartung, and came forward.

"*Pobre, pobre Doctor*," she exclaimed. The news of the kidnaping and the arrests had flown around the village, brought last night by the local *guardia civil.* "Pepe was very worried, said he must go back to town. He'll be waiting at the bus stop. You must have passed him."

Telling her they would pick up the boy and cutting short a stream of abuse concerning Pedro and his evil-doings, "A disgrace to the village, that one, getting honest men into trouble," they said good-by and drove back down the road where they found Pepe at the stop outside the cafe talking with his friend Beppo. His face lighted as the car stopped and he greeted the priest, looking anxiously at the Doctor.

"How would you like a quick trip to the dig and a lift back to town?"

He accepted eagerly, waving at Beppo, who gazed wistfully after them. Too shy to speak to the Doctor, Pepe was glad to see he looked no worse after all that had happened. In the village they reveled in describing his reported injuries, beaten, bones broken, near death. This morning he looked cheerful enough and, turning to Pepe while the priest made a grab at the wheel, "Thanks to you, my boy, Pedro and his pals are locked up, and for keeps. Now we'll see what mischief they were up to at the dig."

Leaving the car at the foot of the hill, they walked through the gate, now swinging open on its hinges, and on up the slope to the empty dig shacks. Here also the doors were unlocked, but inside most of the tools lay as the men had left them and the tables of specimen finds were undisturbed. There was no one about. Pepe, who had never been to the dig before, looked around, reading the dated labels below the rows of pottery and metal bits, wondering about the people who lived and worked here hundreds of years ago. A boy like himself had drunk out of this cup; some woman had scolded her child for breaking this plate.

Satisfied that no great damage had been done, the Doctor picked up a flashlight and crowbar and led the way down the far side of the hill to the caves. Here there were fresh cart tracks, the ground heavily trampled, rocks shoved aside and bushes torn away from the cave entrance. The Doctor crawled inside, motioning the others to follow. Daylight shining through the opening showed marks where boxes and cases were dragged out, and farther in the Doctor's flash traced others in the corner where they had been stacked. Shifting his light over to the cracked wall at the far end, the Doctor crawled forward. He reached behind him for the iron bar and stuck it into the long jagged aperture. The priest and Pepe watched for some minutes as he moved the bar back and forth, hoping to widen the opening, but the rocks held fast. A few more attempts and he managed to pry loose a fragment. Hopefully shining the flash into the hole, he shook his head.

"No good, I'm afraid. The wall's reinforced on the other side. Man did that, not nature. Look at the marks on the rocks. No use our trying to get through today. We'll need special equipment, might even have to dynamite. There's something behind there all right. I was sure before, now I am certain."

The three crawled back out of the cave. The Doctor got up, dusted his knees. "Too bad, I'd hoped we could make it a 'do it yourself' job. Now we'll have to call in expert help. I'll get on to the museum at once, ask them to send some men down tomorrow or the next day."

Father Rodríguez said nothing, only half convinced by the Doctor's certainty. Pepe, his eyes glowing, pulled a dirt-encrusted something from his pocket and handed it to the Doctor.

"This fell when you moved the rock, Doctor."

The Doctor looked, turned the thing over, rubbed at the dirt, and gave a shout. "Now will you believe?" He held it out for the others to see, a flattened piece of greenish stone carved in the shape of a face, eyes, nose, mouth with a protruding tongue. A jade amulet, the Doctor explained, pointing to the small hole in the forehead for a string to pass through. Tenderly tucking it into his pocket, he led the way back over the hill and down to the car.

Euphoric over his discovery, the Doctor burbled happily all the way back to Cuernavaca, reciting dates and details of what he hoped might be found inside the cave.

Pepe listened as the Doctor enumerated various objects, golden crowns, necklaces, earrings, jade mummy cases like those in the Mexico City Museum. He spoke of the fine pre-Columbian collection in Vienna, treasure sent from Mexico to Philip of Spain, part of the Hapsburg inheritance. He told how early collectors had picked up odd bits through the years and, with advancing prices, greedy men had smuggled others abroad. A new find, however, was important, and there was always the chance of coming on something unique and precious.

Father Rodríguez sympathized with his friend's enthusiasm, but he was still cautious. "Suppose this was a single piece, dropped carelessly like the coin?"

Only sobered for a moment the Doctor refused such a suggestion. "That might account for the gold coin, but not for the jade amulet."

As they drove up the Calle Costanza and stopped before the Casa Santa Luiza, the Doctor said, "Present my respects to the Señora. She will be interested to hear about our find. I would go in but I must give the news to my wife and call my friends at the museum." Then, suddenly conscience-stricken, "I was so happy, so excited, I forgot entirely about our lunch. You must be hungry." He handed the package to Pepe. "Don't let me take it home. My wife would scold me."

The Father laughed. "Never mind, Pepe and I will picnic together in the garden." The two got out and Conchita let them in through the gate. Looking at them reproachfully, she informed them that the Señora was resting, so they settled down to eat their sandwiches in a far corner near Pepe's little hut.

After they had finished the priest told Pepe something of the story of Dr. Hartung's discovery of the boxes of drugs hidden in the outer cave and his consequent abduction by Pedro and the two other men, all three of whom were in Gómez's employ. Gómez, he explained, was found to be part of a drug ring whose leaders had now been identified and were awaiting trial in Mexico City. "Your seeing Pedro and his men at Gómez's house gave the police the first hint of their connection with him. They believe that Pedro murdered the man Pablo, fearing he had come to tell me about the hidden drugs. It is a long and very complicated story, but now most of the criminals have been rounded up and you can be pleased to have had a part in it."

Pepe listened round-eyed as the Father went on about the drug traffic itself, the terrible harm it does, and how the Mexican Government was fighting to put an end to it so that wicked men could not profit by bringing such evil into the country and exporting it abroad.

"And the treasure, Padre, did Pedro know it might be hidden in the second cave?"

"I don't think so, Pepe. Probably Pablo just stumbled on

the entrance, noticed the boxes, guessed what they might contain, and came down to tell me about them. As for the treasure, we can't be sure there is anything there until the second cave is opened."

"I did find the green stone, Padre."

"Yes, that made the Doctor very happy."

"It would be wonderful if there was really gold in the cave and all those other beautiful things he told us about."

"Very, very wonderful. We hope that will happen."

Cautioning Pepe to say nothing of what they had talked about, Father Rodríguez looked down the garden as the Señora came out into the patio.

"So there you are, both of you playing truant all morning. You found your family well, Pepe?"

"Very well, *gracias, señora.*"

"Good. There's a box of seedlings just come." She indicated a vacant spot in one of the flower beds, pointing to it with her cane. "You can set them out there, just behind the border."

Turning to the priest, "You look full of news, Carlos. Come and tell me all that has happened."

The two friends sat down in the patio and Father Rodríguez recounted the latest developments, including the Doctor's attempts to open the second cave and Pepe's finding the jade amulet.

"I do hope the dear man will not be disappointed. His heart is set on the treasure. It would be sad if this comes to nothing."

The Father agreed.

"And what a scandal in Mexico City today. My phone rang all morning. It seems that José Mendes has been arrested, charged with heading a drug ring, and others, people everyone knows, are involved. The Mendes family are beside themselves. José has always been a problem, a bad lot from all accounts. What a wicked world we live in, Carlos."

"There has always been wickedness in the world, I'm afraid. Wealth and privilege bring their own temptations and the devil is no respecter of class distinctions."

"You are right, of course, but it is terrible that such people should not exercise public responsibility."

"Unfortunately our own history shows too few disinterested examples."

"The new Minister of Justice is determined to take strong measures on crime of all sorts, drugs especially. I imagine things will go hard with young Mendes. Tell me, Carlos, was that man Gómez part of his ring?"

"I believe so. Rumor says he's left the country."

"And a very good riddance. Poor Dr. Hartung. What a dreadful experience he had. If only things go right at the dig, that will be a compensation."

Conchita brought out the tea tray, set it on the table in front of the Señora. There was a message from Señorita Harris. Could she and Señor Cooper call on the Señora tomorrow afternoon?

"But of course. Tell the Señorita I will be delighted to see them, any time after four."

Talk shifted now to the cheerful subject of Arabella's engagement and the possibility of a wedding in the near future, both she and Father Rodríguez agreeing there was still matter for rejoicing in a dark and troubled world.


The news of Mendes' arrested had indeed brought consternation to Mexican society circles. Impossible to believe a Mendes should be hauled to prison like a common felon. Grandmothers, mothers, aunts, cousins were loudly indignant, and their menfolk, elderly cabinet officers, retired generals, and bankers, brought pressure of every kind for his release. Some few rejoiced at the discomfiture of the Mendes family, so proud of their ancestry and historic attainments, but these were mostly persons snubbed by the old aristocracy. The popular newspapers headlined all aspects of the case. Photographs of the Acapulco villa, accounts of gay parties, pictures of notorious guests, and hints of sensational disclosures filled the press.

The Minister of Justice came under violent attack from the right, but, as other individuals became implicated and evidence piled up, the government was deaf to all appeals. As the public became aware of details of the drug traffic and its far-reaching tentacles, there was immediate demand for investigation at all levels. The Church felt compelled to issue a statement, and doctors and social workers wrote deploring the drug evil. It was remarked that a number of prominent citizens had found it necessay to go abroad suddenly on business, but Señor Morado was satisfied that his department had identified enough men to frighten others. A realist, he knew the traffic flow might only be stopped temporarily, but this was a good start and he was determined to make examples of the wrongdoers no matter how highly placed they might be. He was very grateful to the young American for his help and dispatched a letter to Washington commending the officer for his clever handling of the Mendes affair.


Henry meanwhile was going about his routine business at the embassy finding it anticlimactic after last week's exciting adventures. He did not wish to rush Arabella, so he confined himself to the odd telephone calls, hoping each time she might have reached a decision about a possible wedding date. He'd written his family of his engagement and gave a rapturous description of Arabella's beauty and intelligence and his extraordinary luck in finding such a remarkable girl. Even discounting his lover's enthusiasm, he knew they would be pleased.

He was delighted therefore when she rang up on Monday afternoon asking if he would meet her at the Señora's on Tuesday. He agreed at once, his own desk was clear, and the Ambassador was away, so there was nothing of moment to keep him in the office, certainly nothing of greater moment than a summons from Arabella. To salve his conscience, he would check in with the Cuernavaca police, see how things were shaping up at their end. As far as he knew there'd been no further news of Gómez, and he hoped they'd seen the last of that fine gentleman.

Arabella said she would find her own way to the Calle Costanza as she had a package to deliver close by. So on Tuesday afternoon Henry spent a half hour with the police Captain, filling him in on news from the city, and reported promptly at five at the gate of the Casa Santa Luiza, where Pepe, now an old friend, greeted him cordially.

Arabella had arranged to arrive sometime before. Almost shyly she confessed to the Señora she needed her help and advice, so she had come ahead of Henry. Explaining something of her relationship with her divorced parents, both remarried with new families of their own, she was still reluctant to make a precipitate decision without consulting someone wiser than herself. As far as her engagement was concerned and her love for Henry she had no doubts, but she was not sure, he would like them to be married almost at once, perhaps here in Mexico. What would the Señora advise?

"You do not feel that you should return to New York, have your wedding there?"

"No, señora. I've written both my parents of my engagement, but they are busy people, concerned with their own lives. I've been apart from them for so long I think they would be quite satisfied to have me make my own arrangements. Henry, I know, would like his own parents to be here, but his mother's heart condition would not stand the altitude and they told him they would wait to welcome us at home."

"Then we must consider what is best to be done. Remember you have only known Henry for a short time. You are sure, very sure that he is the one man you love?"

The girl's eyes were steady as she answered. "I am very sure, señora."

"Is there any reason then that your marriage should be delayed?"

"Not really. Henry tells me that he is due for leave, even perhaps for a change of post. He suggested we fly home after our wedding here, see my parents and his, after which he would report to Washington for orders."

The Señora got up, walked down the garden path, then, after a few minutes, came back to sit down again.

"I think your young man is right, Arabella. How would you like to be married here in my garden?"

"Oh, señora!"

"It would give me great pleasure. Just a few friends, or as many as you want to invite."

"I didn't mean . . . I never thought, I . . ."

"That's settled, then, provided Henry agrees."

When the latter came out onto the patio, he found the two deep in conversation. Arabella looked up, her face alight, and the Señora smiled.

"We've been hatching plots waiting for you."

"I'll subscribe to any plots of yours, señora, especially if they include a dark-haired heroine."

"Arabella has promised to play the principal role, and you will be acting opposite her. There may be a part for Father Rodríguez. The scene will be laid here in the garden."

"It sounds as though you were staging *Romeo and Juliet*, señora."

"With a difference. This play will have a happy-ever-after ending."

Henry looked at Arabella, then back to the Señora.

"Can you possibly mean that Arabella and I are to be married here in your garden?"

"That is what I hope. Arabella tells me she would prefer to be married in Mexico rather than in New York. Unless you object the wedding can so easily be held at the Casa."

"Object!" Henry leaned down, kissed the Señora's hand. "You are a true fairy godmother. First you introduce me to this beautiful girl, and then you arrange a fairy-tale wedding for us."

"Good. You've only to set the date. The roses are at their best just now. Don't wait too long." Getting up, the Señora walked down into the garden where Pepe had set out the new seedlings, leaving Arabella and Henry to make their plans.

Both were almost overcome by the Señora's offer. "It all seems too good to be true, Henry. A wedding in this garden, can you imagine anything more lovely?"

"And it's so right for you, Arabella. I don't deserve such luck, but I'm utterly and devoutly grateful. As to dates, don't forget what the Señora said about the roses."

"I'm sure the roses won't disappoint us. I have a girl in mind to take over at the shop. I'll need a week or so with her. Then I must put my own affairs in order, pack my belongings, give up my apartment, buy a few clothes. I'd like to come to you new and shining, Henry. And what about the embassy? Will they let you go just like that?"

"My leave is waiting on the books and this last job is pretty well tied up. Ten days, or two weeks at the most, should see me clear."

Putting their heads together over the little black notebook Henry took from his pocket, they finally settled on a date two weeks from Saturday and, when the Señora came back, submitted it for her approval. She was delighted and immediately began to make plans.

"Would you like Father Rodríguez to play Friar Laurence, potions omitted? I assume you are both Protestants, but he is very friendly with our local rector and often shares services with him."

"But of course," exclaimed Arabella. "Do you think he is at home now? We'll go across and ask him. Dear, dear señora, how can we ever thank you?"

"It's enough thanks for me to look at you. Run along now. You've made me very happy."

The two young people left hand in hand. The Señora sat on alone, thinking of the son and daughter she never had. It was growing cool in the garden, the sun sinking quickly behind the purple rim of the mountains. She looked over to where Pepe was giving a last hosing to the new plants. Calling to him, she told him about the wedding, the roses must be nursed along, the flower beds tidied, the shrubs trimmed, all to be at their best on the appointed day.

Clucking disapproval, Conchita came out carrying a shawl which she put around the Señora's shoulders. "It's too late to sit outside. The Señora will catch a chill."

"I was just coming in to tell you and Marta the news. The Señorita Harris is to be married here in the garden. We've only two weeks to make plans and get the house ready."

Delighted at the prospect of retailing the information to the kitchen, Conchita hurried her mistress inside. The Señora smiled as she soon heard the sound of excited voices. She felt quite excited herself.

Telephone communication with Mexico City seemed especially bad that afternoon. Trying to call the museum, Dr. Hartung twice reached wrong numbers, jiggled the phone and the line went completely dead, then came on again with a loud roar. More jiggling, the line clear at last. Repeating the museum's number, the Doctor waited for it to answer and asked for the Director, Doctor Guzmán.

"Doctor Guzmán not here. No one in his office."

"The assistant, Señor Moresco?"

"No one here today. Museum closed."

Exasperated, Dr. Hartung hung up. Monday of course. Muttering to himself, he turned as his wife came through the door with a loaded tea tray.

"I forgot it was closing day. Can't raise anyone at the museum. You'd think the lazy idiots would be there working instead of roistering in town. Guzmán and his assistant are both out, at the races, playing golf or batting tennis balls, I suppose."

"Here's your tea, Nils. I made you pastry rings. I can't think why they call them Danish, in the States. We have just as good in Norway."

"I wanted particularly to talk with Guzmán, tell him about the cave. It must be opened at once."

"I can't see Dr. Guzmán roistering and he's too old for golf or tennis. He's probably sitting quietly at home poring over his books."

"That's an idea. What's his number? I had it somewhere, here in my desk."

"No, Nils. Drink your tea. If there's treasure in the cave, it's been waiting there for four hundred years and another day won't matter. You look exhausted. Much better call him in the morning."

"But the amulet. I showed it to you. Now they've got to believe me."

"Time enough tomorrow."

"Yes, I suppose you are right. You do make good cake, Helga."

She eyed him as he helped himself to another large slice.

"Never ate your lunch, I suspect."

"I was too excited, forgot all about it. I gave the sandwiches to Father Rodríguez and the boy. Didn't dare bring them home."

Mrs. Hartung shook her head. "You're like a boy yourself, Nils. Now tell me again about finding the amulet. You'll spoil your dinner if you eat anymore of that cake."

Dr. Hartung took the jade from his pocket, set it on the table beside the cake plate.

"It was Pepe, the Señora's gardener boy, who picked it up. It must have lain inside the crack, rolled out when I pried off a piece of rock."

Mrs. Hartung reached over to examine it. The stone felt cool in her hand, an ugly thing really but genuine, she knew; the color and texture were right.

"Suppose this was dropped by chance like the coin? If you ask the museum people down and the cave is empty, what then?"

Her husband took the amulet from her. "Scientists can't afford superstition, but I've a feeling that somehow this is a message and my luck is in. The cave won't be empty." He laughed. "Quite a joke on those drug fellows, missing the treasure for those nasty boxes of cocaine. Did I tell you the police found them hidden where Pedro and his pals were holing out? Serves the rascals right. The old gods don't like evil men interfering with their property. Anything I find belongs to Mexico, to its people to see and enjoy. I must say I'd like to keep this bit for myself—but there it is."

Returning the amulet to his pocket, Dr. Hartung gave a last wistful look at the cake plate, then went slowly upstairs. Helga was right. He was tired, needed a bath and a change of clothes. Just as well he'd not gotten hold of Guzmán. He didn't feel strong enough to put up an argument tonight. Tomorrow his head would be clearer. He'd stand no nonsense. The amulet would convince them. The old gods would see to it.

A very happy young man rode back to the city later that evening. The next two weeks would be busy ones. His desk must be cleared, bills paid, packing done, and loose ends tidied up before turning over to a successor. He'd not dared say too much to Arabella about the new assignment the Ambassador had spoken of. Henry had been long enough in the service to know nothing was certain until your orders were written and in your hand, but the job mentioned was a good one, Paris. Paris in the spring, chestnut trees in bloom, delicious things to eat and drink, your best girl on your arm, what could be a better start for married life? Her eyes had sparkled when he told her of the possibility, though he warned her it might be a dream, darkest Africa or the outback of Australia instead. She'd laughed, said she'd even take pygmies or kangaroos as long as they were together. What a girl!

Early next morning Henry got on to García at the Ministry of Justice.

"What's the latest news on the Mendes case?"

"We've pulled in three more of the gang, big shots too, one of them so frightened he's turned state's evidence. The trial is scheduled for next month. The government is behind us and public interest is building up."

Disappointed at hearing that Henry was leaving Mexico, he congratulated him on his engagement and approaching marriage. "We owe you a big debt. I'd hoped you'd be here for the final show."

"Mine was a small part. Very glad I could be of help."

"That tape recording did the trick. We are all very grateful."

"What about Mendes?"

"Kicking up no end of fuss, as you can imagine. Pretends he's repenting his sins, but he'll be in for a sentence, let off after a year or so, I suppose, and go abroad. I think we've seen the last of him here."

"No news of that fat fellow Gómez?"

"No, we've written him off."

Sending his respects to the Minister, Henry urged García to come to Cuernavaca for his wedding, an invitation the latter accepted with enthusiasm.


Luckily for two Mexican gentlemen Zurich banks rarely ask questions of their depositors, provided identity is properly established. In midmorning the two men entered the bank, presented their credentials, and managed to withdraw substantial sums from their numbered accounts. They returned to their hotel and ensconced themselves in a far corner of the barroom. Here they were joined by a younger man carrying a brief case from which he took papers and spread before them. Soon all three were deep in conversation.

That morning the Paris *Herald* had featured news under a Mexican date line of a Señor Mendes' arrest and the discovery of large seizures of drugs, followed by a roundup of persons involved, many of them prominent in Mexican society and business circles. No names were listed except for that of Mendes.

"What a fool to let himself be caught."

"They'll not dare hold him for long," remarked the second man.

"I'm not so sure. Morado is on the warpath. He'll make an example of him, been waiting for this for a long time."

The second man shifted uneasily in his chair, looked over at the third.

"Hope you're right about Swiss extradition laws, Duprez."

"Have no fear, monsieur. So far I have not lost a client. You are both safe here. I advise you to take up residence, however, a villa on one of the lakes, a chalet in the mountains if you prefer, live quietly. These storms often pass over. If not, life in Switzerland has much to recommend it." The Swiss lawyer shrugged his shoulders. "Many would envy you the opportunity of enjoying Switzerland's hospitality."

"Fishing in the lake, gathering wild flowers in the hills! Golf club greens are rural enough for us. We are businessmen, Duprez."

"Our golf clubs are few, and exclusive, monsieur. For the present I would not suggest your applying for membership."

"And our women," broke in the first man, "they would go mad. They live on clothes, bridge, and gossip."

The young Swiss made no comment except, "I have here a list of properties for rent. I will leave them with you. If any of them seem suitable, I am at your service to make the arrangements." He rose, bowed, and left, brief case in hand.

The two Mexicans looked at each other, then got up and walked slowly across the room to the bar.


A big man sitting alone at a table laid down his newspaper and looked out over the harbor. He wore an ill-fitting cotton suit, bought that morning, already rumpled and stained where he had spilled coffee. His hand trembled. The weather was hot and humid, the air heavy with the smell of oil hanging over the waterfront, and there was the pounding noise of dredges from the offshore well digging.

Motioning away the ragged urchin who came by with a shoeshine box, the man lighted a cigar, rolled it around in his mouth, and watched a couple of fishermen unloading their catch, which spilled out onto the cobbles of the quay.

Dumped here like the fish in this small southern port Luis Gómez chewed on his cigar, laid the mangled ruin in his coffee saucer, pulled himself out of his chair, and walked slowly away from the cafe, around the corner, and up a narrow street. From an open doorway a slatternly girl made a gesture of invitation, but the man passed without looking at her, lumbered along toward a building whose drooping flag marked a Post and Telegraph office.

"Any messages for Gómez?"

An indifferent clerk thumbed over papers on the counter.

"No, señor."

The big man turned away, walked out again.

So much for friends, men he'd made and broken. Now they were finished with him, finished with Luis Gómez.


When Dr. Hartung finally reached the museum director, Dr. Guzmán's response was disappointing. Even the news of the finding of the amulet produced little interest.

"I agree that your evidence, pottery shards and metal bits show signs of early habitation. The caves were probably used for shelter in bad weather. I don't mean to discourage you, but single objects, such as coins or odd pieces, often turn up in these places. Sorry we can't send someone down, but we're shorthanded at the moment. Moresco is off to Yucatán tomorrow. Perhaps we can arrange something when he gets back. Bring the amulet along next time you are in town. We'll be glad to take a look at it."

And that was that.

Dr. Hartung put down the receiver and spluttered some round Norwegian oaths to his wife.

"You can't blame them, Nils. You believe in the treasure but you've been digging for months now with little result. You know they were polite last time they came to the site, but we hadn't much to show them."

"All right. I admit it. But now . . . now, I am very sure."

"Better then that you open the cave yourself."

"Open the cave myself? How can I do it alone?"

"The police Captain. You remember he promised to help, to send some of his men up there with you."

"Policemen on a dig. What use would they be?"

"More use than those rascals who kidnaped you, and a lot more honest. If you do find something they won't run off with it."

Only half persuaded, the Doctor finally agreed to telephone the police Captain. The latter listened patiently as the Doctor told him of finding the amulet, proof there might be other objects of value hidden in the second cave. Unable to break down the wall himself, he needed men to help him, especially if it should be necessary to use small charges of dynamite to blast an opening in the rock face. After that he would take charge, as any items found must be carefully handled, broken pieces collected, sorted, and examined. If, as he hoped, the find proved to be an important one, guards would have to be posted until the material could be brought down from the site. The actual opening of the cave ought not to take long, but if there was treasure there they must get inside.

"I can probably spare you a couple of men tomorrow." The Captain's tone was indulgent. He didn't mind helping the old boy out. He'd had a rough time. The men might think it quite a lark and if, as he suspected, the cave was empty, no harm done. If they found anything so much the better.

"I'll clear this with my superintendent and let you know this evening. If he approves I'd like to send my sergeant along. He's done road construction work and could handle the blasting for you. I'll tell him to pick the stuff up and any tools he'd need."

Stammering his thanks, Dr. Hartung called to his wife and told her of the Captain's offer, then began to make feverish preparations for the expedition next day. She must come with him, Father Rodríguez too, if he was free. He'd ask the Señora for her boy Pepe. The team must start early to assemble material from the work sheds and be ready when the police detachment arrived.

That afternoon Dr. and Mrs. Hartung called on Señora Martínez, who was delighted to hear of the discovery of the amulet and the Doctor's new hopes of finding treasure hidden in the second cave. He regaled her with the story of his adventures, and she was horrified to think of his ordeal and of the part the man Gómez had played. Happily the man was gone from the neighborhood and his house deserted and sealed by the police.

"After this, my friend, you deserve all the luck that can come. Certainly Pepe can go with you tomorrow. I only wish I might be there myself, but I'll be waiting eagerly to hear the results."

Father Rodríguez came in as they were talking, and agreed to be one of the party. "I'll bring Pepe along in my car. If you need another hand perhaps we could pick up his friend Beppo in the village." He laughed. "We'll make an odd team of archaeologists, the police, a priest, and two garden boys, but we'll do our best."

Dr. Hartung waited impatiently for word from the police Captain. The latter finally telephoned, apologized for the delay, the Superintendent had just returned from the city. If it was still agreeable he had permission to report with his men at the dig site next morning. Calling Father Rodríguez, the Doctor arranged for his party to set off early to prepare for the others' arrival, so shortly after eight o'clock the Hartungs drew up at the Father's door. Mrs. Hartung had agreed to come along and was armed with an immense basket of provisions.

"The last time, Nils, you let Father Rodríguez and Pepe go hungry, besides policemen have big appetites and furthermore, if there's anything to be found up there, I can help with the sorting and packing."

The Doctor was in fine fettle, very sure his hopes of treasure would be realized at last. Father Rodríguez, still dubious, said nothing to discourage him, and Pepe, the amulet hero, felt on the edge of more adventure. Picking up Beppo in the village, they climbed to the dig and began to assemble the necessary equipment for the task ahead.

The police arrived. The men were a cheerful lot, obviously considering this more of an outing than anything else. They unloaded their gear, piled it into a barrow the boys had brought down the hill, and followed them up to where the others waited at the cave entrance. Here the men gathered in a group while Dr. Hartung explained the problem at hand, suggesting he and the Sergeant go into the first cave so the latter could take a look at the wall and decide how to tackle its removal. Unless absolutely necessary blasting should be avoided. The second cave might prove small and it was important that anything hidden there be found intact.

The two men crawled into the cave. Pepe would have liked to go with them. Perhaps his turn would come later. He told Beppo of finding the amulet, but Beppo was more interested in the policemen's talk than stories of artifacts. After some minutes the Doctor and the Sergeant reappeared, the Doctor very pleased the construction man did not think any blasting would be needed. Motioning to the second policeman, a big, strong-looking man, the Sergeant selected tools and in they went. The Doctor, very nervous, waited outside, then walked over to stand by Father Rodríguez.

The big policeman crawled out once to pick up a tool.

"It's coming, señores. Not long now."

The sun was very hot. The little group moved over into the shade. Only the Doctor remained by the cave.

Finally the Sergeant stuck his head through the entrance. "We're through now. Don't know if the hole's big enough. Want to take a look?"

Eagerly the Doctor got down and crept into the cave. The men had succeeded in dislodging some of the bigger rocks and the Doctor's flashlight shone into the second cave, where he thought he could see two or three ironbound chests off in one corner, then the glint of gold spilling out from a rotted wooden box. Now to get through the opening. He could just reach an arm and shoulder inside. That was all. But the treasure, it must be the treasure. How to get it out. He turned to the Sergeant.

"Any chance of breaking down the rest of the wall?"

"Very tough going, señor. Afraid we'd have to blast."

"Tell that boy Pepe to come here. He's small, perhaps we can squeeze him through."

It was a tight fit, but with considerable squirming and pushing from behind Pepe managed to worm his way in. The Doctor handed him the flashlight. The floor of the cave was damp.

"There's another opening up above, Doctor." Pepe picked a trailing vine from a crack overhead and a tiny stream of water trickled down.

"Never mind that, boy. Look over in the corner."

Pepe crawled forward, took hold of one of the chests, pushed it along and through the wall opening.

"There's two more here, and stuff lying on the ground."

"Wait." The Doctor could hardly speak for excitement. "They're getting some bags. Hand the other chests out, put all the rest into the bags. Careful how you handle it. Don't miss anything. Stuff the crack up overhead before you come out. The place might flood."

The Doctor watched, shouting directions as Pepe lifted out the ironbound chests, then went back to make a pile of the gold from the broken box, sifting it out from the sand and dirt on the cave floor. Taking a last look around to make sure nothing was overlooked, Pepe shoved the filled bags through and little by little edged himself out.

Mrs. Hartung had rushed down to one of the sheds and came back with a ground sheet on which the Doctor, with Father Rodríguez's help, set the chests and bags. Kneeling down, his hands trembling, the Doctor fumbled with the rusted locks. They held fast. Picking up a hammer, one of the policemen leaned over, knocked them loose, and the Doctor raised the lid of the first chest.

The hot sun glinted on bits of golden ornaments, tiny figures of gods and animals, rabbits, frogs, and birds, beakers with snake-entwined handles, platters, and drinking cups. As the men watched, the Doctor lifted each object out, naming them as he laid them down.

"These are whistle-shaped lip plugs and here are jade ear spools, hollowed out to insert flowers or jeweled dangles." He held up a small stone head. "Very early. Almost the same shape as those big Olmec heads found in the jungle. Later than those, of course, but curious the type should have persisted."

The next chest held more pieces of carved stone and milky white jade strings of beads and a quantity of pierced amulets like the one Pepe had found. From underneath the stone and jade the Doctor lifted out a gold necklace, a shimmering string of snail-shaped shells, each with drops attached.

"Look, look, Helga. You remember there is one like it in Washington in the Bliss collection, but this is even finer." Laying the necklace down, he said, "It's almost too much, more, more than I could have hoped. I think I'm afraid to open the third chest, and there are the bags." The Doctor sat back on his heels.

"There are no ornaments in the bags, Doctor, only gold coins," said Pepe. "I made sure when I filled them in the cave."

"Those can wait, then," Mrs. Hartung intervened. "Enough excitement for the moment. I'm going to feed you now." Telling Pepe to call Beppo, she directed the boys to bring up the lunch baskets. The Doctor was reluctant to leave his treasures, but she insisted and the whole party moved into the shade. The good lady distributed her sandwiches, unpacked bottles and glasses, handed them around, and everyone joined in toasting the Doctor. Pepe too came in for applause, quite enough to compensate for his scrapes and bruises getting in and out of the cave's opening.

The Doctor, almost too excited to eat, cast longing eyes at the third chest. He got up before the others had finished, said a word to Father Rodríguez, and together they walked back to where the various objects lay spread on the ground.

Hesitating, as if to ask, What more is left for me to find? Dr. Hartung lifted the lid. No glint of gold here, only a carefully wrapped bundle, yards of old rotted cloth, which he unwound and then held in his two hands, the greatest treasure of all, a mask of clear green jade, strips of stone shaped and linked with gold, a death mask for an emperor.

Speechless, he looked down, then up at the priest. This beautiful thing, so rare and precious. With a feeling of humility rather than triumph he asked, "What can I have done to deserve this?"

Father Rodríguez said nothing, content that his friend's hopes should finally have been so richly rewarded. Mrs. Hartung had come over to stand beside the men. She too was silent, but she put her hand on her husband's shoulder, as, very tenderly, he rewrapped the mask and laid it back in the chest. None of the others, the police, the two boys, could know enough to appreciate its beauty and value. Let them look their fill of the glittering gold, but right now this jade marvel would remain his private joy.

It was Father Rodríguez who finally spoke. "You must put all this in a safe place, my friend. It cannot be left here, even under guard."

"Yes, Nils, the Father is right. But what must be done with it?"

As if coming out of a trance the Doctor murmured, "I

don't know, I don't know. The museum . . . closed by the time we could get it there."

The two Hartungs looked helplessly at one another.

"Perhaps the police can help," suggested Father Rodríguez. "I could call headquarters from the village, meanwhile everything should be gathered up and packed away."

Calling the Sergeant over, Father Rodríguez explained his intention of phoning the station in town. Obviously relieved, the man agreed he and his men had no wish to take responsibility for the find's safety. Much better it be turned over to the proper authorities. He would send the boy Pepe into the village with the priest. He would know where to find a telephone, then, if the Doctor chose, he could ride back to town with the treasure in the police van; one of his men, a good driver, would follow in the Doctor's car.

The priest and Pepe went off, the former cautioning the boy to say nothing to anyone they might meet. After the usual struggle with the local operator Father Rodríguez finally got through to the police station, spoke to the Captain, then to the Superintendent, to whom he explained the problem. The latter promised to get into immediate touch with one of the main banks and arrange for the treasure to be temporarily housed in its vaults. As soon as the van returned to town he himself would accompany the Doctor to the bank.

By the time the Father and Pepe got back to the site, the treasure had been assembled and packed. All hands had turned to, the chests had been securely roped shut, and the hoard of coins taken out of the old bags and put into a stout wooden box. The men gathered their gear together and the party started down the hill, dropping off picks and shovels in one of the sheds at the dig.

Señora Martínez had suggested that Beppo come back with Pepe to help in the house and garden, for there was much to

do to put all in order for the wedding two weeks hence, so
the two boys rode home with Father Rodríguez. Beppo, of
course, had decided to become a policeman. Pepe listened to
his chatter, but his head was filled with all he had seen, the
beautiful golden objects and the carved stones.

In the police van Dr. Hartung sat beside the Sergeant,
the third chest at his feet, the rest of the treasure locked
into the rear. He said little, still dazed, marveling at the
glorious fulfillment of this hopes, grateful they had at last
been realized in spite of the discouraging doubts of the
museum authorities, and, he suspected, the unexpressed
doubts of many of his friends. Now the search was ended.
Much, of course, remained to be done, the identification and
cataloguing of the objects and their eventual disposition. The
treasure would stay in Mexico, but it was his find; nothing,
no one, could take that from him.

When they arrived at the police station, the Superintendent
was waiting and they drove at once to the bank, a gray
stone building on one of the main squares. Here they were
admitted by a side entrance. Dr. Hartung got out and watched
as the chests were handed down along with the wooden box
and loaded onto a trolley. Walking behind with one of the
bank officials, the Doctor saw the treasure safely stowed into
the vault, the steel doors shut and locked. The bank manager
wrote out a numbered receipt, handed a duplicate to the
Doctor, who shook his hand and thanked him, apologizing
for the inconvenience of opening the vault after hours.

"It was nothing, an amateur archaeologist myself, I am
glad to be of service."

The police Superintendent drove the Doctor back to his
house, where they found Mrs. Hartung much relieved to hear
the treasure was safe and locked away in the bank. Thanking
the Superintendent profusely for his help, the Doctor handed

him an envelope. "Please give this to your men. They did a fine job, especially the Sergeant. We could never have managed without him." Cordial good-bys were exchanged. The police car drove off and the Doctor and his wife were left to talk of the day's events and the happy culmination to all their dreams.

Next morning Dr. Hartung called the museum Director. Incredulous at first, Dr. Guzmán grew almost hysterical as Dr. Hartung enumerated the various objects found the day before.

"Where are they now? What have you done with them?"

Reassuring the Director of their safety, the Doctor explained he had deposited the lot in a local bank preparatory to their delivery to the museum. Arrangements were then made for a car to be sent to Cuernavaca two days hence. The Doctor would accompany the treasure to the city and remain to oversee its examination, classification, and any needed work in the museum's laboratory.

Satisfied, exhausted, but triumphant, Dr. Hartung and his wife spent a quiet morning. That afternoon they called on Señora Martínez, who was delighted to hear of the great find and much entertained by the description of Pepe's part in it all. She congratulated the Doctor and rejoiced with him on the realization of his hopes.

"Your friends will be so interested. You must be sure to be here for the wedding on Saturday week."

The Doctor promised to return from the city to attend that all-important function, and Mrs. Hartung offered any help that might be necessary.

"I think we have everything pretty well in hand. Arabella and Henry are such nice young people. We are all so happy for them."

The great day finally arrived. The two boys, Pepe and

Beppo, had worked hard in the garden all week, transplanting, clipping, cutting. Vacant spots were filled in with pots of bright flowers, vines were trimmed until finally all was ready for the Señora's inspection. She complimented them on what they had done and the boys felt very proud. From the patio a path led down between the flower beds to a background of deep green where an altar was set up flanked by banks of white roses. The Señora stood by as Conchita came out with a lace cloth and old brass candlesticks to put on the altar, and went back to bring the long satin-covered kneeling cushion to be laid at the foot. The Señora straightened the cushion to her satisfaction, nodded to Conchita, and the two women walked back to the house.

Marta's kitchen was a hive of activity that morning. Kettles simmered on the stove for the helpers' lunch, pastry baked in the oven was cut and set to cool on a marble slab, and mounds of sandwiches were being prepared for the afternoon reception. Caterer's men came to put up long tables beside the pool, crates of bottles were stacked behind, and glasses unpacked and lined up on the tables. Everyone crowded into the kitchen when the baker's van arrived with the wedding cake, a magnificent tiered creation, set reverently to one side until time to be brought out and cut by the bride.

The hour for the service was four o'clock. Soon after lunch Arabella arrived with Mrs. Harvey. Conchita showed them into the room next the Señora's and helped Mrs. Harvey take the wedding dress from its long box and lay it out on the bed, a Mexican wedding dress of sheer tucked muslin crossed with bands of delicate lace insertion.

Arabella gasped. "This isn't the one I tried on. We never carried anything like this in the shop."

"I know, my dear. The others do well enough for the

tourists. It's my present to you. I was glad to find it, for the woman only makes one or two a year and this happened to be the right size."

Tears in her eyes, Arabella threw her arms around the good lady, then looked up as the Señora came into the room followed by Conchita. Conchita, for once smiling broadly, handed the Señora a package wrapped in blue paper. From it the Señora unfolded a white mantilla of gossamer-thin lace and held it out to Arabella.

"This belonged to my husband's mother. She was very beautiful and her son grew up to love pretty women. I know he would be happy to have it worn by you today."

"Dear, dear señora. How can I thank you?"

"Don't try, my child. Just see, Mrs. Harvey, how well it goes with your lovely dress. Conchita, bring me the comb from my drawer, the high one." When the comb was set in Arabella's hair, and the old lace arranged to fall over her shoulders, the three women agreed the finishing touches had been put to the bridal costume.

"Pepe asked to make your bouquet himself," said the Señora. "We thought white roses to match the mantilla. Now I'm taking Mrs. Harvey into the garden. Henry and his best man, that nice friend from the embassy, have arrived and are with Father Rodríguez. Henry sent this over to you." She handed Arabella a small sealed package. "We'll leave you now and be back when it's time for you to dress."

Arabella sat down, turned the package over, broke the seal, and opened it. Inside a flat leather case lay a necklace, chains and loops of seed pearls clasped by a round medallion, with earrings to match, very old and very delicate. How could he have found anything so right, so perfect with her dress and the Señora's mantilla?

The jewel case in her lap, she sat on for some time in a

happy daze, then got up. She must bathe, put on the fresh new underthings, and be ready when the Señora and Mrs. Harvey returned.

In the garden the guests were gathering, colleagues of Henry's from the embassy with their wives, several from other missions including the Frenchman, Jean Bertrand. Henry owed him something for his introduction to Mendes. Knots of local friends surrounded Dr. and Mrs. Hartung to congratulate them on the Doctor's spectacular find. García, from the Ministry of Justice, arrived with a large bouquet sent with a note from the Minister himself. The police Captain attended in his best uniform, and Pepe opened the gate to the American Ambassador, who drove up in a fine beflagged car.

The mariachi band, off to one side, supplied music for the occasion, this by Arabella's request. The Señora, elegant in floating gray chiffon, greeted the guests, then, shortly before four o'clock, went up to stand near the altar, as it was she who would give the bride away.

Promptly at four Arabella stepped out into the patio, where her bridegroom was waiting for her. Henry thought surely she must be the loveliest bride in all of Mexico, radiant in her white dress, her eyes shining below the lace of the mantilla. He took her hand as a blare of trumpets preceded the wedding march, and together they walked slowly up the flowered path to the altar, where the pleasant-faced American clergyman stood beside the tall form of Father Rodríguez, a Spanish saint from an old picture book in his white cassock. The service began. The Señora stepped forward, the best man produced the rings, and, at the end, Arabella and

Henry knelt as Father Rodríguez pronounced the final blessing.

The happy couple were soon engulfed by well-wishers. Waiters appeared with trays of champagne. The Ambassador proposed the health of the bride. The wedding cake was proudly carried out by Pepe and Beppo, and, from his study wall, Father Rodríguez produced an ancestral Spanish sword with which Arabella must cut the first piece. This she did as the band struck up another trumpet fanfare.

Afterward, on the terrace, Arabella opened the dance with Henry. Dr. and Mrs. Hartung waltzed happily together as others followed. Tony Farrar, the best man, partnered Mrs. Harvey, then whirled away with a pretty blonde. Everyone enjoyed themselves. It was a gay scene until time came when Arabella tossed her bouquet into the throng, luckily to be caught by the blonde, and she and Henry disappeared to dress and leave in a shower of rose petals and rice.

The sun was lower now. The guests drifted away; the band, still enthusiastic, played them out the gate, then retreated to the hospitality of the kitchen. The caterers packed up their wares, and soon all was quiet in the garden.

Suddenly very tired, the Señora walked back into the patio. Father Rodríguez followed her and the two friends sat together, scarcely speaking to each other. The shadows grew longer, the mountains dulled to a deep blue gray, then faded into the gathering dusk. It was very still in the patio as the stars came out and the moon rose, clear and cool, shining down as always over the good and the wicked, the winners and the losers, on old age and youth, lovers and children.

Cuernavaca's question remained, the eternal question of life itself. Only the mountains, the moon, and the stars knew the answer.